Lock Down Publications and Ca$h
Presents

I0637419

BAD B*TCHES WIT' GUNZ 2

LIVIN' LAWLESSLY

Written By
Christopher "Diesel" Hornezes

First Edition 2025

Printed in the United States of America

Lock Down Publications
P.O. Box 944
Stockbridge, GA 30281
www.lockdownpublications.com

Like our page on Facebook: Lock Down Publications
www.facebook.com/lockdownpublications.ldp

Stay Connected with Us!

Text **LOCKDOWN** to 22828 to stay up-to-date with new releases, sneak peaks, contests and more…

Like our page on Facebook:
Lock Down Publications

Join Lock Down Publications/The New Era Reading Group

Visit our website:
www.lockdownpublications.com

Follow us on Instagram:
Lock Down Publications

Email Us: We want to hear from you!

Acknowledgements

Hard work, dedication, resilience, and a lot of haters is the motivation anyone with a dream will have. You can't impress everyone, and you shouldn't try. Stay true to yourself, but keep your Higher Power first, then your loved ones. Never give up because nobody will go as hard for you as you go for yourself. To all the ladies that have chosen to become a fan of mine, I thank you from the bottom of my heart. To the guys, I thank you all too. Every one of us has a story inside. Whether we choose to put it on paper or keep it and either use it to teach others, bestow upon them knowledge, or to keep us grounded, we all have one.

God bless all of y'all. Even all you hating-ass bitches that rooted against me, snitched on me, felt like I would never become an author. Guess you were wrong, huh? Mamahuevos.

Thanks again to Ca$h, LDP, big ups to ALL the authors under LDP, and to those who are now doing their own thing. To my brother, TROUBLESOME, mad luv fam. You believed in me, and you kept me hungry for this. Thank you, bro.

To my brother Braylan, my sister Stephanie, my stepdad Steve, my G-ma Carol, Auntie Tonya, Little Miss Lead Foot, Queen Naija, Shorty Duwop, Native Girl, Guera, China, Crazy Legs, Papa, Prince and Princess G Ball, P Real, mad love, yo.

To Tara, Charmayne, Uncle David, Eddie, Mary, Dee, Little, Demetrius, I love y'all. Rest in Peace to my mother and father.

And last, to my heart, my queen. Mattie, I thank God for you every morning I wake up and before I go to sleep. I meet a lot of women, beautiful, good head on their shoulders, but I have never met one like you. I never will either. I love you, mi amor. Dios te bendiga, mamita. Para siempre, nena, mi corazon es tuyo.

Chapter 1

"Come on! I don't have all day! Choose, dammit, or you can all die!" Webster stated, getting fed up with waiting for the two gorgeous Illinois State Police officers, that were in the same narcotics division he and the group of others were in. They were all suited up in tactical jumpsuits like SWAT team members.

Yvette glanced over at the handsome and hood rich dope boy she was so hopelessly in love with, tied up next to his homeboy.

Benicio was dead. His head had been reduced to pieces of skull fragments and brains, splattered all over the floor where he lay, after Webster knocked the Colombian drug lord's shit back with his AR-15. He had been the girls' good friend, job source, and occasionally their wild fuck buddy that did not lack in the freaky department.

Now he was gone. Yvette and Julie, and the two men they had given their hearts to, were surrounded by cops seemingly more crooked than they were.

"Okay! You all die!" Webster said, raising his gun back up and pointing it at T.G., while the others pointed at Bucks, Yvette and Julie.

"Wait!" shouted Julie, as she and Yvette still clutched their own AR-15's.

"I'm done waiting, Officer Tran! You and our dear Officer Jones had your chance!" Webster said, glaring at them. "All I asked for was a date with Jones! I'm not a bad guy! I'm a good guy, goddammit!" he declared, getting pissed at the thoughts of how Yvette laughed at him and clowned him for thinking she would ever go out with a guy like him. "I hate stuck up whores!" he added.

"Hey, Webster." Yvette spoke, taking her eyes off T.G., looking at the tall white boy that made her think of Zack Morris, from the ancient TV show *Saved By The Bell.* "No woman in the world would ever go for a lil' punk ass biatch like you! You are a fuckin' lame, and I bet yo' dick is the size of a bird beak!"

Julie busted out laughing. "Naw, Yvette! That muhfucka the size of an inchworm, Joe! On 'erythang!"

T.G. and Bucks couldn't help but chuckle. In such a fire situation, the beautiful police ladies were clowning the guy who seemed to have everyone's lives in his hands.

The other cops in Webster's dirty crew tried to keep from laughing. A few snickered, while others hid their smiles and grins.

"That's it! You're dead, cunt!" Webster snapped, turning his gun on Yvette.

"Hey. One more thing, Webster," Yvette said, staring death right in the face. "We've made our decision on who dies."

"All of you!" Julie shouted right after.

The door suddenly exploded into a million pieces and a flash bang was tossed in. Yvette and Julie ran and jumped on T.G. and Bucks, covering their eyes and ears.

Before Webster and his team of crooks had the chance to duck or run, the flash bang exploded, immediately immobilizing them all.

"What the fuck, Yvette!" T.G. grumbled, laying under her.

"Nigga, I just saved yo ass! Shut the fuck up wit' that extra shit!" she shot back, as three dogs ran in and went on the attack.

The three-year-old Belgian Malinois jumped on one of the men on Webster's side as he tried to get up. He chomped down on the man's arm and went insane, trying to rip it out of the socket.

The two eighteen-month-old German Shepherds that ran in right behind the Belgian Malinois went straight for Webster. Seeing them through his dizzy vision, Webster tried to run but tripped and fell. The two German Shepherds got on his ass like two hungry wolves on a lost hiker, knowing he had endangered their humans.

Two men in masks ran in right as the other cops all attempted to get up and grab their guns. They pointed their AK-47's and started firing, aiming at heads, not bodies.

BRRRRRR! BRRRRRR! BRRRRRR!

BRRRRRR! BRRRRRR! BRRRRRR!

"Care to tell me what the hell is really goin' on, JuJu?" Bucks asked, as Julie remained on top of him, shielding him.

"What's goin' on is I'ma smack the fuck out 'cho ass for leavin' me, and not lettin' me explain. But for now, shut the fuck up!"

Bucks immediately stopped talking.

In mere seconds, Webster's crew were laid out on the ground, blood pouring out from so many holes left by swarms of NATO rounds. The man that the Belgian Malinois had a strong lock on tried like hell to fight the sixty-three-pound K9 off.

BRRRRRR!

A tug on one of the choppers splattered his head all over the wall closest to him. The dog let go as the headless man fell and spewed blood from the stump where his head had been.

"Call them off! Come oon, call them ooooff!" Webster begged in excruciating pain from one of the German Shepherd's teeth and strong jaws clenched down as hard as possible on his dick, while the other had his teeth sunk into Webster's right arm.

Yvette and Julie got up. They muscled T.G. and Bucks up, then yelled at their dogs.

"Sir!" Yvette yelled to her dog.

"Rock!" Julie to hers.

They released Webster obediently. With bloody muzzles, they ran to their humans' sides as obediently trained from when they were pups.

"Ranger! Come!" the smaller of the two masked men called to the Belgian Malinois.

T.G. and Bucks were so confused by the whole situation. After they found out that Yvette and Julie were Illinois State Police Officers, while on vacation in Kingston, Jamaica, the two big timers left them and immediately went into survival mode. They sold everything linked to their names, cleared their bank accounts, and got rid of their phones. They went underground. For way too long, they had been rocking with the ladies, to not know something that was crucial information. They had robbed, killed and moved large amounts of dope with the girls, and now they had no clue if it was all to set them up or not.

***

Yvette looked at the biggest guy of the two masked men. He looked at her and Julie.

"You two okay?" he asked, sounding like a concerned father.

"Thanks to you, sir, and to Lieutenant Sikes," Yvette told him. "Another two seconds later, none of us would be here."

Yvette and Julie's lieutenant, Jarvis Michaels, pulled his mask up, revealing his dark-chocolate clean shaven face, with a pencil thin mustache. He had been in the department for just over thirty years. To many, Lieutenant Michaels was by the book, but when it came to officers in his squad, the fifty-six-year-old reverted back to when he was handling people on the street, before he even thought about becoming a cop.

Walter Sikes, a tall thin white man in his late thirties pulled his mask up. His low-trimmed beard was reddish-brown like a ginger person. He was in charge of the K9 unit, and had been looking to recruit Yvette, Sir, Julie and Rock into his squad. He wasn't one for breaking the law he took an oath to uphold, but like Michaels, if you fucked with any of his, he and his trained killer were coming for you, with no mercy.

***

"Just be glad those distress apps work," Sikes said. "And you can also be glad that your dogs were at the station already."

Lieutenant Michaels looked at T.G. & Bucks. Yvette and Julie went to untie them. Julie, being extra careful not to inflict any more pain on Bucks than he already felt from getting shot twice at a block party in the Tivoli Gardens garrison of Kingston, used her petite body to help him up.

The two dope boys stood and looked at the two high-ranking cops. They half expected to be cuffed up. They expected the other half to end up looking like the others, laid out in pools of blood.

Webster groaned in pain from the bite wounds. Sir, Rock and Ranger, all stood by their humans, not barking, nor growling, but locked on to him, ready to finish him off if commanded to get him. "You two owe these young ladies," Michaels said to T.G. and Bucks. "Way I see it, you get your heads out of your asses and realize that if they were setting you up, you would already be in Statesville or Menard with multiple life sentences."

"But," Sikes chimed in, "since you aren't, you should probably thank these two, instead of hiding from them?"

Sikes turned to Michaels. "What do you want to do with that cocksucker, Jarvis?"

"I am very certain that our dear lady officers want to handle him themselves, right ladies?" Michaels asked Yvette and Julie.

The two smirked with diabolically evil thoughts for Webster in their minds. They both turned their heads and looked at the man.

"That's a big ten-four, sir," Yvette said with a Grinch that stole Christmas smile that made Webster come close to pissing himself.

***

Tied up, gagged and stashed in the bed of his own pick-up, Webster's heart pounded in his chest, as the sound of the Hellcat engine under the hood of his Dodge Ram TRX roared. He couldn't see a thing, due to the fiberglass cover mounted over the bed.

Behind the wheel, Yvette pushed the Hellcat pick-up hard through the night, to where she had in mind to handle the man that had tried to take her heart from her, but she wasn't the only one that wanted him.

Riding shotgun, T.G. sat quietly, still unable to process what was going on. His mind was so jumbled up, wondering if any of it was really happening.

In the back, Sir and Rock sat on Julie's left. To her right, Bucks sat just as quiet as his homeboy in front of him.

All was silent. Only the big, supercharged Hemi under the hood could be heard. Nobody knew what to say. The elephant in the Ram had the tension in the cab so thick that a plastic knife could cut it.

An hour west of Antioch, Yvette entered the property of an old, closed-down meat processing plant in Rockford. Parked by the entrance door, a black Hummer and a big body

Audi A8. Yvette parked the pick-up by the two vehicles and killed the engine.

"Do I have to worry about you still bein' here after we're done with this bitch ass cracker?" Yvette asked T.G., who was looking at her through a new set of eyes.

She couldn't help but to smile at him, seeing in his eyes what she saw before the whole ordeal in Jamaica.

"You're comin' in too, right?" Julie eyed Bucks, daring him to say no, fist balled up in case he actually did.

He groaned to himself. "Doesn't look nor sound like I have much of a choice."

"Smart man. Let's go," Julie told him.

***

They got out with the dogs. Yvette went to the driver's door of the H2. The window rolled down, revealing a man with fair skin, a neat beard, and long cornrows. Three others were inside the Hummer. They all nodded at Yvette, acknowledging her presence.

"Thanks for comin', Rue," she said to the Columbian behind the wheel. "I know this was unexpected for your night."

"Ain't shit. All I want outta this is to see that bitch ass Guero bleed for killin' my cousin," Rueben said, irate to have learned of Benicio's murder. "These honkies is gettin' outta hand, Joe. I finna take over Benny and represent for him, but I need y'all with me still."

"We ain't goin' nowhere, baby." Yvette held the key to Webster's Ram up for him. "All yours, that engine will bring a nice chunk of change."

"Fuck chunks of change, Yvette. A nigga like me wants piles of hunnids, you dig I'm sayin'? I finna be twenty-one years old next week. By the time I'm twenty-two, I need to have at least half a billion in bags that I can touch."

Yvette smiled at him. "You sound just like him. Care to watch some bad bitches wit' gunz work?"

"Nothin' would make me happier," then to his homies, he said, "Vamos a ver muere a este cabrón blanco, my niggas."

Ruben and his guys got out of the H2 and followed Yvette to the TRX.

Off to the side, Julie stood with Sir, Rock, T.G. and Bucks.

"Who are they?" Bucks asked, watching the young Colombian coke boys follow Yvette.

"The one with the braids is the little cousin of the man you were tied up with. Big Colombian family, lots of coke, and lots of clientele."

"I can't believe you hid all this shit from me, JuJu! Like, for real, Joe! What else is you hidin' from me?" Bucks asked.

"I would sure love to know what Yvette's hidin' from me, too," T.G. added.

"Julie! JuJu!"

The three looked as they suddenly as they heard Yvette screaming. Julie took off running towards where Yvette had the tailgate of the pick-up down. Sir and Rock were right with her. T.G. and Bucks ran with Julie on instinct, to see what Yvette was freaking out about.

Julie saw the look of horror on Yvette's face. The looks of rage on Rueben's face, and the faces of his guys told Julie that something was very wrong.

"What happened?" she asked Yvette.

"H-he's gone! Webster's gone!" Yvette panicked.

"Gone?" Julie looked into the bed and saw that a panel to the back of the Ram's cab had been opened up.

She glanced up to the driver's side of the pick-up and saw the driver's door was open.

"Fuck!" Julie shouted, freaking out.

She and Yvette hurried to grab a rag from inside the pick-up and wiped up the blood that Webster lost on the surface of the bed. Holding it to Sir and Rock's noses, they gave their dogs Webster's scent, then released them to go find the wounded runaway.

"How in the hell did he get out of the restraints?" Yvette asked as the dogs ran off in the direction Webster's scent led them in.

"Who fuckin' knows!" Julie snapped, running to get her AR from the pick-up.

Yvette ran and grabbed hers and prepared to go hunting for a dirty pig. "Yvette!" Rueben shouted, halting her.

She turned to face him. "I swear to God, I'ma find him, Rue! On my momma I am!"

He tossed her the key to the Audi. "Make sure that you do. I'll be waitin', but not for too long, I hope."

Yvette took off to catch up with Julie and the dogs. T.G. and Bucks stayed back, Bucks in no condition to run. The two watched the Colombians hop back into the HR and the TRX. They took off seconds later, disappearing up the entry path.

Yvette and Julie returned close to ten minutes later with their dogs. They looked pissed.

"He is gone. No way he got away on foot. We aren't far from the road," Yvette said.

"I bet someone stopped to help when they saw a wounded cop on the side of the road," Julie added, "and they will very likely regret it."

"We gotta go. Come on," Yvette told them all.

They piled into the Audi then. Yvette mashed the gas and flew out of there, hopping onto the highway and headed north. Only when she made it out of Rockford, did she pull out her phone and make the call that she knew wasn't going to go well.

"What's up, Jones?" Lieutenant Michaels answered on the second ring. "You take care of it?"

14

"Uh… so… please don't flip out on me, sir," Yvette said, feeling her heart beat down in her ass. "But, um… he sort of, like, got away."

"What?"

Chapter 2

"Webster is a ten-year veteran in the department, with five years in Waukegan's department," Michaels said to them, from the open window of his Lincoln Navigator, parked next to them at a gas station on the corner of Green Bay Road and Yorkhause Road in Waukegan. "He's going to know every single way to avoid being caught, and he will definitely know how to play offense. It might be a good idea for you two to take some time off."

"Sir, with all due respect," Julie said from the rear, out of her window. "Fuck that silver-spoon Zack-Morris-looking motherfucker. We don't tuck our tails, don't live in fear. He is not stupid enough to retaliate immediately."

"He'll regroup first," Yvette interjected. "He knows how we get down, so he won't come for us until he is sure he can win."

Michaels took a deep breath, then exhaled. Squeezing the bridge of his nose, the lieutenant groaned, not liking the situation in any way.

"This can't get out. We're all screwed if it does, ladies. You know what this all means, right?"

"Painfully!" Julie added, already visualizing inflicting as much pain as she could on Webster, for all that he had done.

Michaels looked into the Audi. He cast T.G. and Bucks the type of look that a father gave to guys wanting to take his daughters out on their first dates.

"Anything happens to them, I'm holdin' y'all responsible," Michael told them. "You won't have to worry about no jail cells either."

The lieutenant pulled off, exiting the gas station, leaving Yvette and Julie relieved that he didn't go apeshit on them, but feeling horrible for not being on point better. His ass and Sike's ass were on the line, just like theirs.

"At least we know Webster won't snitch," Julie said as Yvette pulled off, heading towards Beach Park, where she and Julie lived.

"He'll go down too, if he did." Yvette knew. "We just gon' have to be ready for this cracker whenever he feels like he's ready to try us."

***

Yvette turned into the driveway of her and Julie's two-story home. It sat on a side street in a circular cul-de-sac end, amongst several other homes. It was a quiet area, not even close to the wildness of Waukegan and Zion.

She parked behind her money-green metallic BMW X. Next to it was Julie's white Range Rover Supercharged, done up with custom black exterior accents, sitting on blacked-out twenty-three-inch rims.

"You two are staying with us," Yvette told T.G. and Bucks.

"Naw, Yvette, we gotta—"

"Nigga, what I say?" she snapped, shutting T.G. up quick. "Y'all asses got snatched up by a cracker with a hard-on for us! Fuck you think will happen if he finds y'all again?"

T.G. shook his head. "Whatever, man."

Julie snickered to herself while Bucks remained quiet.

The four of them and the dogs got out of the car. The door to the two-car wide garage rolled up when Yvette hit the button on her keychain. Inside, the two custom Rolls Royce

Cullinans, bought for them by Benicio, sat gleaming under the ceiling light.

They headed into the house, closing the garage behind them. Yvette and Julie fed their dogs and gave them fresh water. Yvette then took T.G.'s hand and pulled him up the stairs to her spacious bedroom. Julie took Bucks to his.

***

In need of a shower, Yvette stripped out of her tactical jumpsuit and boots. Sitting on her bed, T.G.'s eyes went wide as he drank in the thick, pancake-syrup complexioned beauty's five-seven frame.

The twenty-seven-year-old was unbelievably gorgeous. She had the body of a Black goddess, with a model-like face, and full juicy lips. Her long wavy black hair hung down her back, and she was tatted up like a tattoo magazine model.

T.G., a tall, dark and handsome thing that had a resemblance to the rapper Lil' Baby, was a year younger than the badge-wearing gangstress. He and his mans Bucks had been rocking with Yvette and Julie for a few years now, making major moves in the street. The whole time though, neither T.G. or Bucks had known that Yvette and Julie were state troopers, until a near-death experience in Jamaica.

Trust was hard to develop as it was between people. T.G. and Bucks had been successful in the game because when it came down to it, they trusted no man and they trusted no bitches.

Yvette looked at T.G. and saw him staring at her like she was a sizzling T-bone steak, and he was fresh out of prison. Her body was so cold and had his mouth watering. Despite how pissed and betrayed he felt, he loved her, and he needed her, right now.

He got up off her bed and went to her. Yvette smiled as he pulled her to him, into his strong arms.

"Still mad at me?" she asked, flirtatiously.

"Yup," T.G. said, then leaned down and pressed his lips to hers, making her knees get weak and her legs tremble.

Yvette's soul was set on fire by his touch. His lips, his tongue, had her so hot that she felt like she was going to melt. Her nipples grew erect, and moisture built between her legs. She craved him so badly at that moment.

T.G. pulled back as she had come so close to creaming her panties.

Yvette licked her lips at him. "I got somethin' that you can take yo' anger out on," she told him "Come shower with me, and you can beat it up til the hot water turns cold."

T.G. grinned at the idea of wild hot shower sex with the baddest bitch in the world.

"Lead the way, baby," he told her, dick hard and throbbing in his Purple Label jeans.

***

SMACK!

Bucks' head snapped to the left.

"JuJu... if you hit me again, I'ma throw yo' Chinese ass out the window," Bucks told her, turning back, and looking down at her.

SMACK!

Julie fired his ass up again, then she smirked at him.

"I'm Vietnamese, goddammit! Get it right!" she demanded.

SMACK!

Julie, also twenty-seven years old, stood five foot seven as well. She was taller than the average Vietnamese chick and had a petite athletic body. Her breasts were perfectly mouthwatering. She had a slim waist, wide hips, thick thighs, and a round ass. Her long silky hair reached nearly to her ass, and she was tatted up. Amongst her tattoos, what people noticed most was the heart with wings over her chest. Her creamy light brown skin was virtually flawless, despite all the fights and shootouts she got into, all too willingly. The exotic Asian belle was more of a goon than the average chick from the hood. She and Yvette came up in Chicago. Their whole lives, before they became cops, had been spent in the trenches out south and west.

Bucks was almost as light skinned as Julie. His brown hair was cut in a fresh fade, and his low-trimmed beard was neatly lined. He was a little bulkier than his homie, and stood a few inches taller, at six-two. Bucks was more the quiet type. He let things play out first when situations arose, then he stepped up, booted up and ready to get on gangster shit.

***

The twenty-six-year-old started smiling at Julie. She curled her lip and folded her arms over her chest, smacked her lips and rolled her eyes.

"Fuck is you smilin' at, dude? Ain't shit funny!"

"You're sexy as hell when you mad, baby," he told her.

"Oh, now I'm yo baby again, huh?"

Bucks got up and put his hands on her hips, looking down into her eyes.

"You been my baby, JuJu."

"Ain't nobody tryna' hear that shit, Bernard!" Julie shot back, calling him by his government name. "You left me hanging in Kingston, dude! Fuck outta here with that cappin'-ass shit you doin' right now!"

Bucks leaned down and kissed her lips, loving the way they felt against his.

"Don't kiss me again, asshole," she told him.

He kissed her again.

"Stooooop, Bucks! I am fucking mad at you!"

Bucks leaned in again, and this time kissed her with a lot of tongue. Julie moaned, getting weak at the knees, losing all her control, pissed and horny at the same time. She wanted to beat his ass, then ride his dick. After he busted his nut and she got hers, she wanted to slap him, then make him eat the pussy until his face looked like she dunked him in a sink full of water.

"I love you, JuJu," Bucks told her between their kiss.

"Fuck you," Julie moaned as her temperature rose sky high.

Bucks undid her tactical jumpsuit and worked it off her body until it was around her ankles. He scooped her up and tossed her onto her bed and quickly got her combat boots off, tossing them, then pulling her jumpsuit all the way off.

Julie scooted up on the bed and gazed at him while he stripped himself from his Fendi swag, all the way to his boxers.

Bucks licked his lips at the sight of her in the sexy green lace bra and panties she had on. Everything about her screamed sex. His dick grew so hard inside his boxers that it threatened to bust through the buttoned crotch hole of his Tom Fords.

"Drop 'em," Julie demanded, unwilling to deny her arousal any longer.

Bucks obeyed. His throbbing cock stood erect, pointing right at her, pulsating, ready to slide up in her wetness.

"Come here and put this dick in yo' mouth," he told her.

"Make me," Julie fought with a sly smirk.

"Bitch! Bring yo' muhfuckin' ass here and suck this dick like you know you want to!"

Julie's pussy got even wetter by the way he asserted his hood nigga dominance. In a jiffy, she was up off the bed, dropping to her knees before him, mouth opened wide.

Bucks gripped his cock at the base and slid it into her mouth, eyes rolling to the back of his head from the warm wet feel of it.

"Shit," he cursed when Julie took him to the back of her throat with ease. "Goddamn, baby! That's what I'm talkin' about! Suck this dick, bitch! Get all of it in yo' mouth!"

Julie's freak mode kicked in as he stretched her mouth out, the tip of his dick down her throat, past that dangling thing Cardi B demands that a nigga's dick be big enough to touch.

***

Yvette cried out his name, as T.G. held her up against the wall, driving into her relentlessly. He filled her up with his anaconda, nailing her to the marble-tiled wall in her glass sliding door shower. Yvette's legs were wrapped around him, as her arms wrapped around his neck. She moaned in bliss as he gave her the dick she had been without for a whole seven days. She could feel herself ready to explode.

The hot steamy water poured down on the two of them from the ceiling, making it seem like they were gettin it on in a tropical rainstorm, outside a temple somewhere in the Amazon.

Bucks made her explode a minute later. Yvette came all over his dick. She demanded he hit it from the back right after.

He let her down, spun her around, and smacked on her double bubble booty. Yvette leaned over, poking it out, looking back at him. Bucks smirked, then dropped down behind her, and buried his face in the crack of her ass.

Yvette bit her bottom lip, eyes squeezed shut, relishing the sensation of his tongue swirling around her puckered asshole. He slurped and sucked on it, kissing it like it was her lips. He knew he had some ass kissing to do in order for his queen to forgive him, for ghosting her like a punk, instead of handling it like a real man. The only way to kiss ass was to eat ass, and it helped that T.G. loved eating ass.

"Ooohhh! Tremaine, you a nasty nigga!" Yvette cried out as she rose up on her tippy toes.

T.G. blew on her asshole, motorboating it. Yvette shrieked from the vibration that his lips made, then she climaxed, squirting his chest.

He got up and slid into her soaking wet pussy from the back and went savage on her. T.G. gripped her hips and worked her hard and fast, with powerful strokes that had her seeing stars.

Yvette pushed him back enough so she could bend all the way over. She grabbed her ankles and gave him all phat juicy bubble. T.G. gritted his teeth and kept pounding her until they both got ready to cum.

She came first, erupting like the volcano that burned up the people of Pompeii. T.G. pulled out of her, his dick seconds away from exploding. Yvette turned, dropped, opened her mouth and let him fuck her face until he was empty, and her mouth was full of his hot globs of semen.

Yvette moaned, playing with his cum. She spit it out on his dick, then she slurped it all back up and swallowed it, licking her lips clean.

"Still mad at me, Tremaine?" she asked, being helped up from the shower floor.

"Naw, how can I stay mad at the baddest bitch on earth?" he told her, putting his arms around her. "Especially when she let a nigga go crazy on her whenever he wants."

Yvette busted out laughing at him. "Good. Now let's wash up and get some sleep. Tomorrow's a big day, we got business to handle, and for the meantime, fuck the law."

T.G. laughed. "Seems to me that livin' lawlessly is what you and JuJu do best, love."

"You know it. So, toughen up, nigga, 'cause shit finna get real crazy, real quick."

***

Julie screamed out at the top of her lungs as she came all over Bucks' dick. He clenched his teeth, holding her hips, laying on his back with her on top. Seconds after she came, he came, nutting inside of her.

"Woooo!" she started, feeling so very satisfied.

"You ain't mad me no more, right?" Bucks asked, looking up at his sweaty freak.

SMACK!

"JuJu!"

Julie busted out laughing at him. She fell over sideways, rolling like she had inhaled laughing gas.

Bucks rolled on top of her, pinning her down with one hundred ninety-seven pounds of hard body.

"Why you keep smackin' me?"

"Because you deserved it."

"Past tense?" he asked.

"Sure." She smirked at him.

"Julie Tran, I'm really gon' fuck you up, shortie! Wit cho' Cambodian ass!"

She tried to smack him again, but his hands were wrapped around her wrists, holding them down.

"Uh huh! Now what? Fuck you talkin' bout, shortie?" he teased.

Julie smiled at him, then in a flash, pulled a move that was so fast that Bucks didn't even realize he was on his back on the floor for nearly five seconds.

"What the fuck you just do to me, JuJu?"

She laughed at him, "I just treated yo' ass, foo'!"

Her phone started ringing just as she was about to continue taunting him. Thinking it had to be Lieutenant Michaels calling, Julie jumped up and ran to get her phone from the side pocket of her jumpsuit. But when she saw that it was a random number, she thought it was another officer in her squad.

"Tran," she answered.

"You thought it was gonna' be that easy to get me?"

Julie's heart dropped when she heard Webster's voice.

"Yeah. Your heart dropped, right? The sound of my voice scares the shit out of you."

She looked at Bucks. He saw the look of horror on her face and hurried to her, his eyebrows furrowed, seeing how bothered she looked.

"Don't worry, Tran. You don't have to say a word. I'll speak," Webster said. "You and Jones are on borrowed time. You will lose sleep, thinking about when I will pop up on you. And there's nothing you can do to stop me, you little egg-foo-young loving cunt!"

Julie started seeing red from the racist comment.

"By the way, you and that nappy-head monkey deserve a Porn Star of The Year award, especially you, slapping him right after you got done riding his cock."

The call ended. Julie gasped.

"What happened, JuJu?"

She took off running to her closet and came out with an AR-15, loaded with a mini-drum, running naked out of the room, down the stairs, to the first floor.

Sir and Rock heard her and ran from the kitchen to the living room, where Julie was hurrying to get the front door unlocked and opened.

"JuJu!" she heard Bucks yell as she ran outside. Ignoring him, she saw a SUV parked in the middle of the street. It was a huge SUV, bigger than what she had ever seen before.

The headlights turned on. The engine revved and a second later, it shot forward. Julie raised her gun and started firing at it. Sir and Rock barked viciously at the vehicle.

She clenched her teeth and kept shooting, having no intentions of sending, all one hundred rounds of 5.56mm slugs at it.

It swerved to the left and hopped the curb, coming right to where she stood with the dogs. Bullets started flying at it from above just then.

Suddenly, a pair of hands yanked her back, right before the big Rhino slammed into the Audi, hitting it so hard that it flipped over and hit her Range Rover.

Sir and Rock got out of the way just in the nick of time before the massive, armored SUV's huge wheels could crush them.

***

Yvette and T.G. heard Bucks yelling for Julie as they got out of the shower. Right away, Yvette went to her closet and got her M4 carbine. T.G. hurried and grabbed an AK-47, slapped a hundred-round drum in and ran with Yvette to the window.

They both saw Julie blasting at a big vehicle, while she stood naked behind the rear of the Audi, with the dogs. They both took aim at it when it swerved and charged right for Julie.

Yvette squeezed the trigger and started dumping at it. T.G. let the chopper spit, aiming for the windshield. None of their bullets penetrated any part of the SUV.

"Fuck!" Yvette cursed as the thing sped at Julie.

T.G. caught a glimpse of his homie grabbing her and pulling her out of the way seconds before the giant could run her down.

The crash was loud when it hit the A8. The Range Rover's alarm started going off when the Audi smacked into it.

The Rhino came to a stop and stayed where it was. Yvette pointed her machine gun at it, ready to blow the driver down.

"It's no use, bae! Whoever that is ain't gettin' out!" T.G. told her.

Yvette hopped up and ran downstairs. T.G. followed. They got to the front porch right as the SUV reversed, gunning it backwards.

The neighbors had awakened from the gunshots. Many looked out of their windows, others bravely came to their front doors, seeing the truck speed off, leaving a mess.

"JuJu!" Yvette screamed, running to her home girl, relieved to see that she was okay.

She took her robe off and put it on her, not caring that people could see her in her bra and panties. T.G. helped Bucks up. The dogs were at their humans' sides, shaking with adrenaline.

Yvette pulled Julie into her arms, tears falling from her eyes. Julie trembled, enraged by Webster's audacity to come to her home, and attempt to mow her down.

"Aye, Joe! Get y'all shit!" T.G. said angrily. "Y'all comin' with us! Ain't a nigga in the world crazy enough to come to where we been layin' low at!"

Julie looked at him. "Then how did Webster's guys catch you, Bernard?"

Bucks shook his head as his guy's jaw muscles clenched.

"They ran up on us while we was makin' moves," T.G. told her, grinding his teeth in anger. "Dude took half a mil' and seven bricks, too."

Yvette and Julie shook their heads but said nothing. They were known for doing the same exact thing to unsuspecting dope boys.

"It's gon' be aight, baby." Yvette went and wrapped her arms around him. She looked up into his eyes. "I got cho' back. Trust and believe, we won't let you and Bucks get snatched up by the big bad wolf again."

"Yvette, shut cho' ass up and go pack yo' shit, Joe!" T.G. yelled, as Julie busted out laughing. The dogs barked at him as the girls laughed hysterically.

Bucks just shook his head.

"Shut cha'll asses up, goddammit!" T.G. said, then marched back into the house, while the ladies were still laughing like hyenas.

Chapter 3

Yvette and Julie filled big duffel bags with money, drugs, guns, clothes, shoes, and jewelry. Then T.G. and Bucks got the bags into the two Rolls-Royce trucks, just as Lake County Sheriff and Illinois State Police vehicles sped onto the block, responding to the many calls from panicking neighbors.

Lieutenant Michaels hopped out of his Expedition. Lieutenant Sikes hopped out of his Toyota Tundra. They both ran over to where the ladies were garbed in T-shirts, leggings and sneakers. The two had floored it all the way from their homes when the call came in from others on the squad about the attack on their beloved female officers.

Tow trucks came and took away the destroyed Audi, and Julie's heavily damaged Range Rover. While assuring their boss that they were fine, a couple of detectives came to get their statements.

Neither of them gave up anything that would point fingers at Webster. The lieutenants stood by their side, then deaded the questions when they saw Yvette and Julie were on the brink of tears.

T.G. and Bucks stepped in, swearing on their lives that they had Yvette's and Julie's backs. Michaels and Sikes gave them both hard looks, then nodded.

The others from their squad did their own check on Yvette and Julie, before they all began to part ways. T.G. pulled Yvette's glossy white Cullinan out of the garage. Bucks pulled Julie's powder-blue Cullinan out, parking next to Yvette's. They hurried to get the ladies and their dogs inside, then they skirted off, riding both six-hundred-thousand-dollar SUV's like they were meant for the drag strip.

***

Around 2:00 in the morning, T.G. and Bucks made it to the north side of Milwaukee. Arriving at 27th and Atkinson, they bent the corner where a gas station was and rolled down Atkinson. Yvette and Julie saw groups of people out and about still. They were deep, like they were expecting someone of importance to ride through.

Pulling up to a decent-looking house, the two turned into the driveway, and parked in the back where a two-car wide garage sat next to the grassy rear.

Yvette peeped a mob walking up the driveway as T.G. killed the engine.

"Relax. Them all me and Buck's young niggas, bae," he told her, peeping her hand wrapped around her big .357 Taurus. "They hold shit down when neither of us are around."

He opened the door and got out. Yvette got Sir by his leash and got out behind him. Bucks, Julie and Rock hopped out and joined T.G., as the group of young goons and goonettes greeted him.

"Damn, dog, fuck you get a Rollie truck at, bro?" said a tall, slim, dark-skinned dread head, rocking Fendi and a Patek.

"It ain't even mine, it's my girl's shit," T.G. told him.

T.G. and Bucks introduced the ladies to the group of eleven. Learning that the dread head, called G-Lock, was T.G. and Bucks' right-hand, and the other guys and girls were all G-Lock's own goons, Yvette and Julie relaxed a little, which caused their dogs to relax.

"Make it known to erybody that if they see these ladies and them trucks, if a muhfucka even think about tryna' hit a lick on 'em, they gon' die," T.G. told G-Lock.

"Say less, my nig. On the G, ain't nobody gon' fuck wit' cha'lls girls," G-Lock assured him.

***

Inside the house was as decked as a condominium. The outside compared to the inside was like night and day. It was luxury, pure opulence with glossy veined marble floors, imported Italian appliances and furnishings, with a built-in home audio system.

T.G. carried Yvette's bags into the bedroom he made his, with Sir trotting right behind Yvette. Bucks led Julie and Rock into his room, carrying her bags. The women were both majorly astonished by how lush the bedrooms were.

"Okay, then, big baller," Yvette said, nodding in approval of the royal African tones used to create a vibe that said Black Power slept here. "I do believe our dear Madam CJ Walker would've wanted a room like this when she got rich off that hot comb."

T.G. chuckled. "Miss Sarah Breedlove likely had a house with plenty of rooms like this, baby."

"Listen to you! You know her real name!"

"Black History was my favorite subject in school," T.G. told her. "I love my people, and all those that contributed to makin' us all kings and queens."

Yvette smiled. She loved a man that was in tune with his existence on earth. A Black man with knowledge was truly powerful in her eyes.

"I didn't even know that you and Bucks were from Milwaukee, though," she said, unzipping one of the bags with the dope in it.

"Bucks and I didn't know you and JuJu were cops," T.G. threw back at her. "So, I think we're even."

Yvette cast a scowl at him. Instead of feeding into the past, she pulled out a brick of raw heroin, laying it on the bed. She pulled out four more, then she pulled out eight bricks of Colombian cocaine.

T.G.'s eyebrows rose, looking at what he saw as two hundred fifty thousand in dope, and another hundred sixty thousand in coke.

"Well, okay then! I'm guessin'. . . them ain't come from a plug," T.G. said.

Yvette shrugged. "They came from a plug, but we took 'em from the nigga who was plugged."

T.G. busted out laughing at how nonchalant she was about using her gun and badge to get into places that most hardcore gangsters couldn't shoot their way into.

***

Julie pulled out twelve kilos of fentanyl, and eight bricks of ice. Bucks was already seeing dollar signs. Fentanyl was cheap, but the glass-shard-looking crystal meth could bring in up to twenty-five gees a wop.

"You gon' help me get rid of this, right?" she asked him, seeing the wheels in his head already turning,

He nodded. "I can most definitely get it all gone. Got some guys out this way, but it might be easier to dump bulk off in white neighborhoods."

Julie chuckled. "Set it up. Rock and I will be your back up if shit hits the fan."

Bucks got his phone and started making calls. By the third one, he had two keys of fennie sold, and a half brick of ice spoken for. Right as he was about to place another call, his phone rang. "Who this?" he answered.

"What up, bro, this Cheese."

"Cheese?"

"Yeah, nigga. We was locked up together, bro. I had the long wicks and tattoos on my face. You did me right when I came home."

"Oh, yeah. Damn! How you get this number, though?"

Julie furrowed her eyebrows, hearing him ask a question like that.

"My nigga, you just called Lambo. He know I been tryna get back in traffic, so he told me you got gas, bro. What up, dog? A nigga in need out here."

"Where's here?"

"Jamesville. Nigga, muhfuckas is gettin' chicken out this way, but it ain't been that good-good. I need that turn-em-up shit, dog."

"Aight. Gimme a lil bit, I'll hit you when I'm movin' around."

"Bet. Love too, foo'," Cheese said.

"Yup."

Bucks ended the call then. He saw Julie staring at him. "What?"

"Doesn't look like you have much faith in doin' business with whoever that was, Bernard."

"Naw, it's all good. I know dude, he just thirsty and think he the shit, but he stay spendin' money," Bucks told her, then yawned. "I need some sleep, though. I'm drained."

"Well, get some sleep, I'ma go take a shower," Julie told him.

***

Come holla at me in the bathroom

Yvette saw Julie's text and sent a *Be right there* text back.

T.G. was hard at work, weighing dope and coke, bagging up orders that continuously came in. Sir was laid out on the bed relaxing peacefully, while King Von bumped from T.G.'s iPhone.

He was so busy with what he was doing that he didn't notice Yvette leaving the room.

***

She went to the bathroom and entered. The lights were on, steam came from the shower. Yvette closed and locked the door behind her. She kicked off her Air Forces and stripped all the way naked. At the shower, she slid the curtain to the side. Standing there, under the streams of hot water, was Julie.

She smiled, beckoning Yvette into the shower.

Yvette stepped in and closed the curtain. Immediately, Julie grabbed and kissed Yvette, slowly prying her lips open with her tongue. Her hands slid down Yvette's side to her hips, then she cupped her ass. Julie's pussy got so wet by the feeling of Yvette's meaty ass. There was nothing better than a bad bitch with a phat ass, except for a bad bitch with a phat ass that was a motherfucking certified gangstress.

Julie kissed Yvette's breath away. She slipped a hand between Yvette's thick thighs and started playing with the pussy. Yvette gasped when she felt Julie's fingers stroking her clit. Her body responded in ways that only Julie could make happen. They had been lovers on the low for as long as they could remember. From an early age, the two discovered their attraction to women. They experimented with each other in their middle school days, and had been getting intimate ever since, especially when neither of them had some good dick around.

***

"Mmmmm, JuJu... Fuuck, baby," Yvette moaned, as Julie lowered herself down and started sucking on her right nipple. "Oh God, that feels so good!"

Julie sucked Yvette's left nipple, then kissed her way down her flat stomach, until she was on her knees, with Yvette's trimmed box right in front of her face.

She made Yvette raise her right leg, then put her foot on her shoulder. She buried her face in Yvette's goodness gracious, attacking her clit like a savage freak, high off ecstasy. Julie worked Yvette like it was her own pussy, knowing exactly how Yvette wanted it.

Yvette's body shook and trembled. Her back arched, toes curled, asshole clenching and unclenching. Julie made her head spin in circles like her tongue was doing at that moment. A few minutes later, Yvette exploded, splashing Julie in her face.

They flipped the script then. On her hands and knees, ass tooted up, Julie moaned as Yvette sucked on her pussy from behind. She tongued her swollen lips down like they were the ones on her face. Julie nutted in just over six minutes. Yvette ran her tongue up from the pussy, entering Julie's ass crack. She bit her bottom lip hard when she felt Yvette's tongue in her ass. The dirty feeling had her going crazy. She climaxed again, just minutes after her last orgasm.

"You's a nasty bitch, eatin' bootyhole 'n shit," Julie said, as they both stood up, knees weak, legs numb, pussies dripping.

Yvette just tongue kissed her again.

"Just like you eat my ass, Julie?"

"Shut cho' ass up. Ain't nobody ask you all that, ass muncher."

Yvette laughed. "I love you, bitch," she said, wrapping her arms around her.

Julie smiled, wrapping her arms around Yvette, cupping her ass. I love you too, hoe. Now let's go take advantage of our men while they're vulnerable."

"Bet!"

***

After Yvette gave her man a much-needed break to break him off, they passed out, naked and sweaty.

Julie woke her man up and made him take her down, then they caught some well-deserved rest. Around eight o'clock the next night, they all woke up fully recharged and ready to get to it.

Yvette and T.G. got dressed after a quickie in the shower. T.G. sported Ariri with Retro Jordan 5's on his feet, diamond studs in his ears, a white-gold rope chain around his neck, and an Audemar Piguet on his wrist.

Yvette slipped on new pearl-blue Victoria's Secret panties and bra, then put on a blue and white striped Chanel top, blue fishnet pantyhose, with a denim Chanel mini-skirt, and Chanel hoops in her ears. Her hair went up into a high right-sided ponytail, and she put on some Chanel No. 5 perfume. Grabbing her big blue Chanel tote bag, she put her Taurus .357 in it, with her back-up Glock .40 and extra clips, and a hunting knife. She wasn't playing any games.

T.G. got the coke and dope in a duffel bag. With Sir in his harness, they were ready to make moves. Before they headed out, G-Lock came and got two bricks of coke and one brick of heroin to pop off while T.G. and Yvette handled the rest.

***

Swagged out in a black and gray Louis Vuitton fit, with the low-top checkered shell-toe Louis Vuitton sneakers to match, Bucks stood there with his jaw nearly on the floor, when he laid eyes on Julie. She was looking irresistibly good in a straight, long-sleeved leopard-print Balenciaga dress, with black pantyhose, and red T-strap six-inch Red Bottom spike toe pumps. Her hair was flat-ironed, parted up the middle. She rocked gold Tiffany & Co jewelry, with a gold Cartier on her wrist. Bucks took a look at her glossy red lips and swallowed hard, craving to have them wrapped around his dick again.

"Why you always wear pantyhose around me, knowin how I got a fetish for that shit?" he asked her.

"Because it makes you be very sure to make sure nothin' happens to us, so we can make it back safely, and you can fuck my brains out. Plus, pantyhose and diamonds are a woman's best friends."

He laughed. "You make it hard to concentrate."

"Havin' a bad bitch as your business partner is very beneficial, bae." She went and sat on his lap, feeling his hardness poke her in her ass. "Women like me, make lames envy you and want to take me from you. So, they go above and beyond to try to be your friends to do a little 'bizness with you, just to get close to me, then bang! Got 'em!" she shouted, wiggling her booty on him. "We take every single dollar he has and knock his shit back."

Bucks looked up into her eyes, smiling with true admiration. "Since you rescued me from Zack Morris, have I told you that I love you?"

"Nope. Spit that shit out," she told him, batting her long lashes and giving him a seductive smile.

"I love you, Julie. You are the one who I do not want to be without, ever again, bae. Real nigga shit, you's the realest ride or die a nigga will ever have."

"Aww! Bernard! Come here, baby!" she told him, wanting him to raise his face closer to hers.

Bucks lifted his head to get a sweet one, when suddenly…

SMACK!

"JuJuuu!"

Julie screamed out laughing as he rubbed that hot spot on the left side of his face from another open hand. The shocked look on his face was truly hilarious.

"Yo' ass is really wild, shortie," Bucks said, chuckling at how soft Julie made him.

"I know." She leaned down and kissed his forehead. "I love you, Bernard."

"Shut up, punk."

Julie cocked back to smack him again. Bucks caught her wrist before she could.

"Stop, you little devil. We gotta go, so save the violence for whoever acts dumb."

She smiled. "I can definitely do that, handsome," she told him and got up, hollering for Rock while Bucks got the bag and his keys to his whip.

***

T.G., Yvette and Sir got up into the black-on-black SRT-8 Dodge Durango and left. Bucks, Julie and Rock got up into his Hemi-powered Jeep Wrangler Rubicon, sitting up on big off-road wheels with rammer bar bumpers in front and in back. He pulled out of the garage and made his way to get on the road to dump off orders around the north side, the south side, then down to Jamesville.

***

A little over fifteen minutes later, T.G. turned his Durango into the soul food restaurant's lot, on 34th and Fond Du Lac, called Boogie's Best. The lot was filled with vehicles. Everybody wanted Boogie's golden fried chicken, deep fried catfish, and crispy French fries. The owner was known throughout all of Milwaukee for having the best southern cuisine in all of Wisconsin.

T.G. parked next to a sleek black 1970 Cadillac Deville with Boogie Man on the front plate. He reached into the back row, grabbed the bag, and told Yvette to come on. They got out, leaving the engine running, the a/c blowing, and the windows cracked for Sir. Yvette kissed his nose through the window, telling him she'd be back.

***

They entered the restaurant together, making a beeline towards the employee entryway behind the counter. A few of the people in line looked at them, wondering who they were. A couple of youngsters made catcalls to Yvette, but she ignored them, having no interest in even looking at children trying to be men before it was their time.

The two cashiers waved at T.G., with flirty smiles on their faces. Yvette stopped, pausing behind them, daring them to keep on with narrowed eyes. They both turned away, putting their eyes back on the customers.

T.G. led her through the food assembly /prep section, back to where a big, lush office was.

"Aye, ol' man." T.G. knocked on the door, looking inside.

The tall dark-skinned man sitting in a button-tuck leather high back chair turned his head and saw T.G. there. He was a well-known hustler, pushing close to his sixties. His salt and pepper hair was freshly faded, his waves spinning out of control, beard lined sharply, the yellow-gold Rolex on his wrist flicking hard. He was dressed in a casual Gucci polo shirt, with slacks and some wheat Timbs on his feet.

"Shawty, what's up wit' cha?" he said, with a faint southern accent, deep and jazzy like Isaac Hayes.

"Brought you some shake 'n bake for 'dem chickens you fry so perfectly."

T.G. stepped in with Yvette. He introduced her to Boogie, then closed the door behind him.

"Always good to have you a beautiful woman that can have yo' back, youngsta. My wife was mine. She gone, but she ain't forgotten, ya' hea' me?"

"Yes, sir. Loretta was a good woman. I miss her, man," T.G. said, as his eyes went to the big blown-up photo of Boogie and his dearly departed wife hanging on the wall.

"Me too." Boogie smiled at the photo of himself.

Yvette couldn't help but smile at the sentiment filling the office up.

"A'right, Tremaine. Whatcha' brang for ol' Boogie Man, huh?" the old school asked, ready to get down to business.

T.G. pulled out three bricks of dope for Boogie. He picked one up and sliced it open with a knife, digging out a small mound of the light brown powder. He nodded his head as the odor coming from it wafted into his nostrils.

"Talk to me. I get some nice numbers?" Boogie asked.

"That's a question for this beautiful Black woman next to me. It's her dope," T.G. told him.

Boogie turned and looked at her.

"Forty-five each is the best I can do," Yvette told him, not willing to go any lower, even though she and Julie got it all for free.

Boogie nodded his head. To him, forty-five thousand was a great price. He could tell it was uncut, and he'd normally been getting taxed fifty-five thousand and better.

"I can do that price, Yvette." Boogie reached for the phone on his desk, pressed a button and picked the receiver up.

T.G. and Yvette waited. A second later, Boogie spoke.

"Bring me a dolla' thirty-five to my office," the O.G. said, then hung it up.

"While your money comes, Yvette," Boogie said, looking from her to T.G. "I'm wonderin' if you still do a little… side moves, still?"

"When money flows, anything goes, Boog'. You need somethin' handled?" T.G. asked.

"Hol' up a sec, youngin'. I'm gon' let you hea' this clown for yoself."

Boogie got a little black cell phone from the top drawer of his desk. He made a call, putting it on speaker. After five rings, T.G. and Yvette heard a very ignorant answer.

"Man, what the fuck you want, old-ass nigga?" they heard a guy snap.

"I'd like to provide you with one last chance to pay that debt. Thirty-five grand isn't chump change. I've been very nice about it, but my patience has worn thin," Boogie said.

T.G. and Yvette stayed quiet. For close to ten seconds, the line was quiet, until they heard the guy start laughing his ass off.

Boogie looked at them and shook his head.

"Aye, old-ass nigga! Check this shit out, dog! Yo' old ass is beat, fam! Nigga, I ain't payin' you shit! And you can make all the threats you want! This ain't the eighties, dog! Niggas like me run these streets now, ol-ass fry-cook, dip-the-fish-in-batter-and-cook-it-up ass nigga! Come on, man, get cho' washed-up ass up off my line with' that dumbass shit, nigga! You wanna' come holla, then by all means, you know where I'm at! Be careful, though! It's a real zoo out this way!"

The call ended then.

Boogie chuckled to himself.

"That was some very disrespectful shit," Yvette said, feeling her blood boiling.

"Niggas like that deserve to get pistol-whipped until they ain't got no teeth," T.G. added.

"Well, the new generation of young guys and girls, don't think anyone can touch 'em. You see how fucked up Milwaukee is. Even Trump's bitch ass scared to come 'round, talkin' 'bout how bad a city the 'Mil is," Boogie said, shaking his head again. "Tell ya' what though, Tremaine. It's about time them lil' niggas got them some act right. You handle that for me, and I mean real good, you can keep that money."

"Fuck the money, Boog', I'ma handle that off the strength, fam. On God!"

"And I'm with you, baby," Yvette added.

The knock at the door halted the conversation. Boogie got up and went to the door. He opened it and was handed a book bag. Closing the door back, he turned and handed it to Yvette.

"I got a money counter for you to—"

"We're good." Yvette cut his words off. "Sorry to cut you off, but I been around a lot of hustlers and gangsters. I know real, and I know fake. You, sir, are in the top two percent of real, so I have no need to count."

Boogie smiled at her, then looked at T.G. "Nigga, the next time I see you two, if she ain't got a ring on her finger, I'm gon' ask for her hand in marriage."

"And I'ma knock yo' old ass back to Memphis," T.G. joked.

Boogie and Yvette laughed their asses off.

"Be careful though, youngsta', them niggas live by a very different set of rules over in the zoo," Boogie said, giving them fair warning about the infamous Burleigh mobsters.

T.G. and Yvette nodded their heads.

"Anybody can get got," Yvette said then. "Lionesses hunt their prey, catching their meat when it foolishly leaves the group."

Boogie smiled at the two. "I better get invited to the weddin'."

Chapter 4

Bucks followed Highway 11 until it became Court Street. Nodding his head to Nipsey Hussle's "Racks In The Middle," featuring Roddy Ricch and Hit-Boy, he got to Lynn, ganged a right turn, and made his way to the corner of Lynn and Racine.

Julie stroked behind her dog's ears as his head rested on her lap. She surveilled the area. It was quiet, and every house had fences. They were definitely in the hood, but it was far from the type of hood she and Yvette had grown up in.

Pulling up to a two-story house, Bucks peeped that there were lights on in what he guessed to be the living room. He parked two houses down and killed the engine.

He called Cheese and waited for an answer.

"Yeah, what up, bro?" came Cheese's voice from the speakers.

"Come out. I'm here," Bucks told him.

"I can't. I'm on an ankle-monitor, and my daughter's in the bed sleeping. Why you can't come in?"

Bucks shook his head. "Open the door," he told Cheese, then ended the call.

He grabbed his cannon and tucked it in his waistline. Julie went to open her door, but he stopped her.

"Wait here, bae. In case we gotta get up outta here fast, I need you behind the wheel."

Julie looked at him. Rock grunted, as if he was thinking the same thing.

"I do not like this, Bucks. Somethin' don't feel right," she said, climbing into the driver's seat.

"Nothin ever feels right when you movin' kilos, gorgeous. I'm a thoroughbred nigga though. Have no worries," Bucks told her. Then with the two bricks of fentanyl and one brick of ice in a book bag, he left. Walking towards the house, keeping his eyes peeled, and his hand close to his waistline.

***

Julie watched his silhouette get up to the front door of the house. She could just make out a big round guy with long wicked dreadlocks open the door. He dapped Bucks up then invited him in.

Rock growled, getting her attention.

"I know," she said to him, stroking his ears. "We'll be outta here soon, baby. Just be ready."

Rock barked at her then went silent as his protective instincts kicked in.

***

"Come on, man. Fuck you got me walkin' into, Joe?" Bucks said, when he saw drug addicts all over Cheese's living room, getting sky high.

"Nigga, this my spot, dog," Cheese replied with a slick smile. "Don't worry about them. Come on, the office is this way.

Bucks glanced around as he followed the hefty dope man. A few of the meth heads looked at him, eyes wide, looking crazed and frenzied, while the others continued smoking and snorting.

Following Cheese, they entered a small utility room that had a desk with a computer on it. Bucks stopped as Cheese turned and faced him.

"Where's the money at, bruh? I don't got time to—"

Bucks stopped mid-sentence when he felt the barrel of a gun touch the back of his head.

Cheese chuckled as he saw the set-up register in Bucks' eyes.

"Sorry 'bout this, bro, but I don't never pay for my merch," he said.

Cheese walked up, patted Bucks down and took his gun.

"Nice. I'll keep this too, my nig'. The dope, consider it a write-off, you know? A charitable donation."

Bucks grilled him with a venomous glare. "You are a very stupid dude, my nigga."

"Oh, yeah? How is that? I'm not the one that has a meth-head pointing a smack to the back of my head, willin' to blow yo' top off for a hit," Cheese laughed. "Now get the fuck up outta my house before you die."

***

Bucks fumed as he marched out of Cheese's crib, with no drugs, no money, and without his gun. He went to the Jeep's driver's door. It opened as he got to it.

"What happened?" asked Julie, seeing the look on her dude's face.

"Scoot over," he told her, "and get cho' gun out. This nigga got me bent!"

***

"Aye, Molly! I got a hit for you, bitch! Come suck this dick and I got chu'!" Cheese said to the frail white girl, wearing a tattered shirt, short skirt, and beat-up Reeboks.

She jumped right up from the couch, leaving the three other girls behind to go get her some more meth.

"Hey, what about me, Cheese?" Sabrina whined, fiending for a blast. "I'll let you fuck my ass again!"

"Bitch, last time I did that, you shitted on my dick! Fuck outta here! Molly! Bring yo' ass, bitch!"

Cheese turned his head to his bedroom, when just then, bright lights filled his living room. The roar of an engine came. The fiends in the living room screamed.

Cheese turned back around, just as he saw the big Jeep speeding right at his house.

"Oh shit!" he panicked, just as the mini-monster truck crashed right into the living room, crushing three people that were too slow to get out of the way.

***

"Wooooo! That's what the fuck I'm talkin' about, baby! Yeah!" shouted Julie, when they came to an abrupt stop in Cheese's living room.

Bucks laughed and hopped out with his Glock, popping a man that attempted to run at him with a knife. Julie let Rock out and got out with her Night Hawk 1911 .45 semi-auto, dumping at anyone that wasn't Bucks. She blew at another guy that was having a fiend episode, rushing at her with a broken glass bottle. One slug in the center of his forehead made him fly backwards and hit the floor, silenced forever.

Bucks heard a loud crash after he slumped another fiend that tried to stab him with a syringe. He craned his neck and caught sight of Cheese making a break for it.

"Yeeaah, nigga! I see you!" he said to himself, then took off after him.

"Bucks! Wait!" he heard Julie shout, but he was gone, locked on Cheese like a Pit Bull chasing a cat.

***

Cheese pushed his way out of the rear door to his house, using his two-hundred-eighty-five-pound body as a battering ram. Huffing and puffing, he ran for dear life towards the fence at the rear of his backyard. He heard endless gunshots and screaming inside his house. Making it to the fence, he sighed in relief, happy that he was alive, unlike all his clucks.

"Fuck 'em. I'll find more snappers," he told himself, grabbing the fence to pull his heavy body up.

He had gotten just one foot off the ground, when he heard vicious growling, immediately followed by the most excruciating pain in his ass from sharp teeth sinking into his flesh.

Cheese screamed at the top of his lungs as the dog yanked and pulled. The crippling pain made him let go of the fence. He fell backwards onto the ground. The dog had let go to get out of the way, but got right back on him, chomping down on his arm and biting down as hard as he could.

***

Bucks and Julie stood side by side watching Rock make the tough guy cry like a bitch.

"Think he's had enough?" Bucks asked her seconds later as Cheese begged and pleaded for the dog to be called off.

"Hold on. Gotta wait for it," Julie said, with an evil smirk.

"What? Wait for what?"

As soon as he asked, they both heard Cheese fart loudly, followed by what sounded like wet ones.

"Eew, shit!" Bucks exclaimed, wrinkling his nose. "That nigga just pooted, Joe!"

Julie laughed. She called Rock off him and praised him for a job well done. Bucks walked up to Cheese, smelling the foul odor coming from him.

"My man. First off, you stink!"

CRACK!

Bucks kicked Cheese hard in the side of his head.

"Second, you's a dummy."

He kicked him again.

"Now get cho' bitch ass up and take me to my merch. I get my shit back and I won't shoot you in yo' kneecaps."

***

Cheese limped ahead of them. Bucks kept the barrel of his Glock pointed at the back of his head. Julie gripped her .45 with both hands and kept her eyes alert. Rock was on it, his training and instincts had him ready to annihilate any threat to his humans.

Back inside the house, Bucks, Julie and Rock walked past all the dead dope fiends they had blown down. Following Cheese, they arrived in his bedroom. Bucks saw the bricks on the bed.

"I'm good now, right?" Cheese asked, so scared that he was close to shitting his drawers even more.

Bucks turned to get all the bricks back in the bag. He looked at Julie and nodded his head.

Cheese saw it and looked at her. "Naw! Wait! Hold up!" he panicked when she raised her gun up at him. "Don't—"

BOCKA!

She sent a hot one through his left eye, making his head snap back. His brains flew out the back of his head, splattering all over the wall behind him.

His lifeless body dropped to the floor, blood pouring out the back of his head.

"Time to go," Bucks said, then ushered Julie and Rock to the Jeep.

"Freeze! Police!" they both suddenly heard.

"Don't move, or I'll shoot! You! Lady! Drop the gun!"

Julie glanced at Bucks through the open passenger window where she stood. Rock growled at the uniformed cop. He didn't care that the man was law enforcement, he posed a threat.

"Okay! Don't shoot! I'll drop it!" Julie said to the cop.

Bucks started panicking. No way was he letting his woman go down for his move.

Julie already knew what Bucks was thinking. Before he could do it, she acted. She dropped and twisted too fast for the cop to process. She pointed her cannon at him and sent five rounds at him, hitting him in his chest and throat.

"Fuck!" Bucks cursed, as the cop dropped, blood gushing from his throat and mouth.

"Let's go!" Julie shouted, hopping into the Jeep with Rock.

Bucks jumped in, slammed it in reverse and floored it, ejecting the Rubicon from the living room. He spun around and peeled off, hauling ass as the sounds of sirens filled the air.

**

Posted in front of a duplex on Burleigh Avenue, between 13th and 14th, the mob of young gangsters and hustlers were turnt up, clowning around, high and drunk with some chicks at their side, ready to fuck and suck for a buck.

Trell, Vernon, Racks, Devaugh and Cezar laughed at their homie Nook.

"Nigga, on God, that bitch ain't even really related to me! Her thot-ass is my stepdad's niece, dumbass nigga!"

"Don't get mad at me for not keepin' it in the family, Nook!" Ted laughed. "All these hoes out here, and you fuckin' on yo' own cousin! Kevin Gates-ass nigga!"

"How 'bout this? Fuck y'all niggas! I'm out!" Nook declared, pulling out the keys to his 2019 Range Rover Sport.

"Fuck you gon' go do? Fuck another cousin?" Trell clowned.

"Naw, I'm go fuck yo' bitch, lame-ass nigga!" Nook shot back, shutting Trell all the way up, and turning all the laughs onto Trell.

***

Nook hopped up in his Range and pulled off, pissed that his guys were clowning him like a goofy.

"I got somethin' for you to laugh at, Trell," he said to himself, pressing the display screen to bring up the Bluetooth phone dialer.

He went to her number and pressed call. Three rings went before he got an answer.

"What up?" Taisha answered.

"You at the crib?" Nook asked, cruising west on Burleigh.

"Yeah. Why? Where's Trell?"

"Fuck that gay-ass nigga. Yo' boyfriend a punk. I'm 'bout to pull up, though."

"Nook, you know we can't keep doin' this. It's not right."

"Bitch, miss me wit' all that. Ain't nobody tryna' wife yo' ass up. I'm just tryna' get nasty again, and you know you love this dick, so quit cappin' like that pussy ain't gettin wet as we speak."

She started laughing at him.

"Guess you'll find out when you get here, huh?"

"Yahp. In a minute, shortie," Nook said, then ended the call, with a smirk on his face. "I finna' buss' all in this bitch mouth, then make her put that shit on the Gram when he kiss her."

Nook busted out laughing his ass off as he approached Taisha's street.

He slowed down with his right turn signal on and was about to turn, when a hard bump came from behind.

Nook slammed it in park, grabbed his FN, tucked it and hopped out as a chick in a short skirt, and fishnet pantyhose with some Jordans on her feet, got out from behind the wheel of the Dodge Durango that had hit his SUV.

"Bitch, what the fuck wrong wit' chu'? Yo' ass drunk?" he snapped, walking up on the ridiculously beautiful woman.

She started smiling at him as he marched. "My bad, lil' dude."

"Yo' bad?" Nook questioned, getting closer to her. "Bitch! You just hit my—"

CRACK! CRACK! WHAM!

In a blink of an eye, the girl hit him with a lightning-fast one-two-three, sending him stumbling back.

"Fuckin' bitch, dog!" Nook snapped, as a few cars sped past.

He went to up his pistol on her, when suddenly, a man hopped up from on the passenger's side of the Durango's front end, with a paintball gun.

PACK! PACK! PACK!

"Aaagghhh, shit!" yelled Nook, as three frozen ones hit him in his face.

The girl ran up on him while he tried to shake it off. She socked his ass up again, knocking him on his ass. The gun flew out of his hand when the back of his head hit the pavement.

She went and grabbed it, then stood over him with it.

The man with the paintball gun came and stood over him on the other side. Nook looked up at them both, puzzled as to who they fuck they were.

"You're probably wonderin' who we are right now, huh?" the man said, not worried at all about the cars that were passing in both directions.

"I don't know y'all at all!" Nook snapped, feeling dizzy from the girl's fists.

"True. But you know Boogie, and he is not happy with how you spoke to him on the phone. So, you are comin' with us, lil' nigga."

The girl then kicked Nook in his face hard enough to send him off to la-la land.

***

T.G. led the way back to where Boogie had requested the young clown be brought. Yvette pushed the Range Rover behind him, with Sir riding shotgun next to her, as they headed towards Sherman Park.

Pulling into the park, they both cut their lights off and rolled through the grass, towards the little orange light that came from flames under a big pot.

Standing next to it, they saw the old man, waiting for them.

T.G. and Yvette parked. From the back of the pick-up, T.G. muscled the young shit-talker out of the bed, dragging him towards Boogie.

Yvette got out with two .40 cals and Sir, her eyes shifting around, keeping a lookout for anybody feeling the need to be nosey.

T.G. smacked Nook awake. When the youngster saw Boogie, he freaked out. T.G. grabbed him and held him in place.

"What up, Nook, my boy!" Boogie said with a smile. "Didn't think you'd be seein' an ol' fry-cook again, huh! Ya' hungry? I got some fish for you."

Nook clenched his teeth. He was breathing hard, scared shitless, but trying to hold strong.

"See, you know what's wrong with all you lil' young punks?" Boogie asked him. "First off, can't none of y'all fight, y'all just pick up a gun and get to shootin', and most of y'all ain't got no aim. Lil' young kids dyin' every day from stray bullets meant for someone who beat cho' ass or fucked yo' baby momma. What y'all need is to get the baby shit slapped out cha'll asses, but you... ain't no helpin' you. So..." Boogie reached down, turned the fire off, and put on thick gloves. "I'm gon' show you what I love best 'bout bein' a fry-cook," he told Nook.

T.G. then rammed his knee into Nook's lower back. Yvette and Sir watched as Nook howled in pain, falling to the ground. T.G. backed away from him. Boogie lifted the big pot full of boiling cooking grease and walked up to Nook.

The youngster screamed when he saw what Boogie was about to do.

"O.G.! Wait!" he pleaded.

"Nope. Tonight, the Zoo will be short one less animal," Boogie said then he dumped gallons of piping hot Canola oil on Nook's face, the oil immediately doing what it was intended to do.

"Aaaaaaaaaaggggggghhhhh!"

T.G., Yvette, Sir and Boogie all watched the boy flip and flop like a fish out of water. The hot grease burned away his flesh, exposing bone and skull. He rolled over, back onto his back. They could see his bare skull.

His eyes rolled in their direction, then seconds later, Nook took his last breath.

"Hmmm... this makes me want some catfish," Boogie said, averting his eyes to T.G and Yvette. "Catfish, macaroni 'n cheese, greens and some cornbread. Y'all want some?"

"Hell, yeah! We hungry as hell!" T.G. exclaimed.

"Straight up!" Yvette agreed. "And so is my doggy-woggy! Ain't that right, Sir? You hungry?"

Sir barked excitedly, his tail wagging fast and wildly.

"Cool. I got someone'll take that nice SUV the youngin' had. Give 'ya a nice penny for it. Let's get on to my spot and I'm 'on make us some plates," Boogie told them.

Leaving the fried punk where he was, T.G. switched and got into the Range, while Yvette and Sir climbed into the pick-up. Boogie got into his luxurious ol' school Cadillac Coupe DeVille and led them to his restaurant, to chef them up a well-deserved, southern-style home-cooked meal.

Chapter 5

Julie puked her guts up behind the gas station she'd hurried off I-41 to get to, when she started feeling sick. Rock's head hung out of the window. He whimpered, sensing something was wrong.

Bucks held her hair out of the way, while she vomited violently.

"Bae? You cool?" he asked, reaching back to rub her back.

"Yeah, I just … ate something bad."

Julie cleared her throat, then sat up on her knees. Bucks helped her up and scooped her off her feet.

"I'm not paralyzed, Bernard. I just threw up," she said as Bucks carried her to the old Lincoln Town Car they had stolen, after dumping and burning the Jeep.

"I know. I can smell it when you talk."

Julie narrowed her eyes at him. "I'll smack you."

"I know you will, but yo' ass better not."

He got her into the passenger's side and sat her in the seat. Rock climbed up front and sat on the floorboard in front of her. She leaned down and kissed his face, then hugged him.

Bucks hopped back in and pulled off, hopping back onto the interstate, heading north back to Milwaukee, praying there wasn't an APB out for him and Julie.

Julie waited very impatiently for the text she had sent out to be replied to. It was close to 4:00 a.m., so she had not expected to hear back from him until the sun came up.

Bucks got back to Milwaukee and got close to the block. He, Julie and Rock got out. Julie grabbed the bags of cash, while Bucks kept his guns ready. They hurried away from the car after Bucks wiped the inside down.

Making it to the house, the three hurried inside and let out sighs of relief.

***

"Are you serious?" Yvette asked incredulously, after Julie called her and in careful words, told her what happened.

"Very," Julie confirmed, feeling her stomach churning again.

"Goddammit! This shit is gettin' crazy!" Yvette said.

Julie felt Rock nudge her with his nose as she sat on the bed next to Bucks, who was also on the phone. She patted his head and waited for Yvette to speak.

"Okay, Aight. You hit up LT already?"

"First thing I did. He's likely laid out though."

"We'll be there in a minute. Do not leave, JuJu!"

The call ended.

Julie sighed, laying back on her back, clueless as to what the future held. It was not looking good at all.

"If shit can't be done, I'll turn myself in, bae," said Bucks. "I won't risk your life to save mines."

She looked at him.

"Bernard, shut cho' ass up with' all that. You got me all the way fucked up, if you think I ain't ridin' with you 'til the very end, Bernard!"

"Julie—"

"No! Don't say shit else! We gon' make it up outta this situation, then we gon' find that bitch ass cracker and make him scream like a bitch while he gets gutted like a pig!"

"Well damn," Bucks chuckled. He pulled her to him, putting his arm around her. "That was very passionate, baby. Remind me to never piss you off again."

"Don't ever piss me off again, or I'ma punch you in the dick while you're sleep."

Bucks let her go and scooted away from her. Julie busted out laughing at him, and then she felt it coming up. She jumped up and ran to the bathroom and hurled into the toilet.

Bucks sighed. He looked at Rock, who was looking at him.

"Our assistance is needed, Rocky Rock. Come on," he said, then went to help Julie not puke on her hair.

***

"You found him yet?"

Yvette groaned in frustration. "No. Been having to handle some other things, man."

She heard Rueben mutter a curse. He was not happy.

"Maybe you need a little motivation," Reuben then said.

Bright headlights appeared behind them as the driver turned on the high beams. T.G. and Yvette both looked as the vehicle swerved around and pulled up next to them, stopping neck and neck to the red light they had been waiting at.

The pitch-black passenger's side of the Bentley truck rolled down. Sitting there with a poker face on, was Rueben, with a chick behind the wheel. Sir started growling out of the rear driver's side window.

"Nigga, what? You think we supposed to be scared?" T.G. snapped, as Yvette gripped her pistol.

He slammed it in park and jumped out. Reuben smirked as T.G. walked up on him.

"You ain't 'bout that life, my nigga. Hop yo' ass back in that cheap-ass ride before I put killers on you," Reuben threatened.

CRACK!

T.G. cocked back and rocked his jaw.

"Tremaine!" Yvette screamed.

Sir went bananas, barking viciously, his eyes locked onto Reuben.

"Go, bitch! Hit the gas!" Reuben shouted as T.G. kept punching him up.

The girl panicked when blood flew on the right side of her face. She mashed the gas and made the pipes smoke when the V12 engine screamed.

T.G. jumped back, narrowly avoiding getting his feet run over. He wanted to get his gun and send a few hot ones to catch up with it, but too much had already happened.

"Tremaine! Get in the truck!" Yvette yelled, frantically looking around for cops.

Sir was still barking out of the window, grunting and growling.

T.G. watched the brake lights of the Bentayga disappear when it bent a corner. Yvette yelled again, demanding he get in, or she would bestow upon him great bodily harm.

Heated, he ran and hopped back in.

"T.G., what the hell were you thinking?" Yvette demanded to know as he slammed it into drive and pulled off.

"What was I thinkin'?" he asked as the V8 roared. "I was thinkin' that it's gon' be a cold day in muthafuckin' hell, the day I let a bitch ass nigga intimidate my woman! You got a problem wit' that?"

Yvette got real quiet. His words shocked her.

"Didn't think so!" He approached Atkinson and turned. "And secondly, dude is trackin' you somehow. Ain't no way he just pops up behind us on coincidence."

"He doesn't have nothin' of mines, Tremaine!"

T.G. swerved into the driveway and parked the Durango next to Yvette's Rolls-Royce truck and cut the engine off.

"He has yo' number! Any half smart person would know that anyone that's plugged can get yours traced if they have yo' number, Yvette! You's a muthafuckin' cop! Act like it!"

She smacked her teeth. "Shut up, nigga."

He shook his head. "Bring yo' ass, Yvette, before I make Sir get on yo' ass."

"Nigga please," Yvette said back, waving him off, but she got out of the SUV as T.G. demanded, while he grabbed the bags of money and their guns.

**

Inside, they both heard sounds of someone throwing up. Yvette could tell it was Julie. Rock ran out of Julie and Bucks' bedroom when he heard Yvette, T.G. and Sir enter. The two dogs, reunited after a long day, jumped around each other excitedly despite them both sensing their humans' anguish.

Yvette hurried to the bathroom and found Julie kneeling over the toilet, puking her guts up. Bucks was next to her, holding her hair back with one hand, rubbing her back with the other.

"What's wrong with her?" Yvette asked, rushing over to lend a hand.

"She said she thinks she ate somethin' that doesn't agree with her," Bucks told her.

He told Yvette and T.G. what had gone down in Jamesville. Yvette shook her head. T.G. couldn't believe what he was hearing.

"A fuckin' cop, though?" he snapped.

"It couldn't be helped, bro! It was him, or us!" Bucks replied.

"Drug addicts are one thing, Bucks, but killin' a cop? This is not good," said Yvette.

"I killed him," Julie said, wiping her mouth. "Bucks is innocent."

"He's Black, the second he was born, he was guilty," T.G. said sadly. "This is why we left Wisconsin in the first place, man. Nothin' but bitch ass niggas and snakes out here."

"Fam, that's everywhere!" Bucks corrected. "The only difference between Wisconsin and other states is they can legally convict niggas without any evidence! 'Hearsay' is the death of a street nigga in Wisconsin!"

Yvette's phone dinged from a text. She got it out of her handbag and saw a message from Reuben.

You can run but you can't hide! Here comes the BOOM, bitch! LMMFAO! he said.

"What the hell is wrong with this dude, Joe?" Yvette asked out loud.

Before anyone could ask who had texted her, a loud explosion rocked the house. From how loud it was, they could tell it came from the inside.

T.G., Bucks and the dogs immediately got in mode. They demanded Yvette and Julie stay put, then they rushed out, closing the bathroom door behind them.

***

"Shit! These niggas threw a fuckin' firebomb in here!" T.G. exclaimed as flames burned up the living room.

"We gotta get them out of the house!" Bucks said.

They ran to their bedrooms and grabbed their AK-47's, hurried back and got Yvette and Julie out of the bathroom. Smoke filled the entire house. The fire grew bigger every second.

T.G. led the way to get out of the house through the back door, when bullets started flying from the backyard.

"Get down!" he yelled, grabbing Yvette and taking her to the floor.

Bucks grabbed Julie and took her down next to them. The dogs crouched low at their sides. Glass and shrapnel flew as the mob outside continued Swiss cheesing the house.

Yvette choked on the thick smoke. Her eyes burned. She couldn't see or breathe.

"Bro! We can't stay in here any longer or we're dead!" Bucks shouted.

T.G. knew he was right, but from how it looked, they were either going to burn to death or be shot to death.

He looked at Yvette under hm, choking, suffocating, dying. In that moment, all bets were off. He saw red, and not because of the fire. "I love you, Yvette," he said to her, then hopped up with his chopper.

"T.G.!" Yvette hollered, still coughing.

Bucks jumped up and off Julie and clutched his spitter. He locked down at his magnificent beauty. He told her he loved her, then with T.G., they made their way to the door to create a way for their ladies to get up and get out of there, even if it meant that they wouldn't.

***

"Alla! Allaaa! Agarralos!" Reuben shouted, seeing the door fly open.

Twelve deep, his sicarios opened fire. Twelve Dracos spit hundreds of rounds and by the time Reuben yelled for them to hold their fire, he was sure that if bullets hadn't ripped them apart, the fire and smoke had to have gotten them.

He yelled for some of them to go check it out. Staying put where he was, on the side of the garage, with two fully automatic Glocks in his hands, Reuben watched five of his guys advance towards the burning house.

They got to the back porch, when suddenly, they were doused with some type of liquid.

"What the fuck?" Reuben asked as they all looked at each other, tripping hard, realizing they were drenched in bleach.

A man appeared in the doorway just then. In his hand was a burning ball of paper. Reuben gasped when he hurled it at his guys. They all ignited as the flammable liquid caught.

The second man ran out blasting his AK, running to the left, while the other blew his AK while running to the right.

Reuben's hitters were quickly caught off guard by the strategic move. As they dropped like flies, Reuben peeped Yvette, Julie and their dogs stagger out of the house, choking their asses off.

"Fucking bitches!" he spat.

He raised his guns up and took aim at them. He wrapped his fingers around the triggers and fired.

***

"Come on, JuJu!" Yvette yelled, pulling her bestie/lover from the floor.

They heard T.G. yell for them to hurry. Running to get out with Sir and Rock behind them, they made it out, just as T.G. and Bucks fanned down the shooters. Right outside the back door, they saw five burning bodies and all three SUVs were filled with bullet holes. Bucks yelled for them to run to him. T.G. continued exchanging gunfire with the few that remained.

They ducked low and ran towards Bucks. They got to within just a few feet of him when bullets came flying at them, hitting the house, right above their heads. They both grabbed their dogs and hit the ground for cover.

***

BRRRRRRRRRRR!
BRRRRRRRRRRR!

Reuben blew both of his altered cannons, trying to take both cop chicks out. He saw them duck, just in the nick of time, grabbing their dogs and dropping down to the ground.

"Yeah, stupid-ass hoes! Make it easier for me!" he said, aiming at them again.

"I dare you, bitch nigga."

Reuben felt steel touch the side of his head. He cursed under his breath, bewildered to not have seen anyone approaching him.

"No chance in beggin' you to spare me, I bet?" he asked.

"Not a snowball's chance in hell, dummy."

"Didn't think so," Reuben said, then in one brazen effort to live, he dropped to the ground and swung, punching the man in his dick.

***

"Aaghh, shit!" T.G. yelled as the blow rocked his balls.

He fell to the ground in pain, unable to do anything but hold his throbbing testicles.

"Bitch ass nigga! I'ma kill you!" he shouted.

"Nigga, who is you talkin' to?"

T.G. heard Bucks' voice just then. He opened his eyes and saw his guy there, but Reuben was nowhere to be found.

"I just had that little bitch, bro! He hit me in my dick!"

Bucks gave T.G. an incredulous look. "Wow."

Sirens wailing from close by got their attention. They heard Yvette and Julie shouting, yelling for them to come on.

"Yo' ass better not tell nobody about this, bro!" T.G. said as Bucks helped him up.

"My nigga, this is somethin' we all gotta take to the grave," Bucks said, then helped his mans away from the devastation of scattered bodies and three shot-up SUVs.

***

"Wow. They are really something, eh, Sammie?" said Bernice, from the passenger's seat of Samantha's BMW MC. "I don't think I've ever run across anyone in my career that's been involved in so many murders and shootouts in a twenty-four-hour span."

Samantha looked at her partner and lifelong friend. "You must have forgot about the Valdez family, huh?"

"No, but these four are just plain lucky," Bernice said.

They watched as the two female Illinois State Police Officers, their murderous dope-dealing boyfriends, and the two German shepherds hurried away from the burning house, leaving behind what looked like a news report of another attack in Israel and Iran, all of them on foot.

"Well, their luck won't last long," Samantha then said.

She reached out to the dashboard and brought up the screen for the phone. She selected her husband's number and pressed call.

It rang four times before he answered.

"What do you want?"

Samantha curled her top lip up, disgusted with the man. She couldn't remember a single reason that allowed her to marry him.

Bernice just shook her head, glad that she didn't do relationships, nor marriage.

"They're on the move," Samantha said.

"You're telling me this, why? I'm not the one that wants to make them do my dirty work and demand that I let them live!"

Samantha ended the call on his ass.

"Fucking prick."

"Hey. How about we make a quick stop at that place on 34th and Fond Du Lac? I could go for some Boogie-fried chicken!" Bernice said, licking her lips.

"You can do whatever you want when I drop you off." Samantha pulled off from the curb, turning her lights on. "I'm gonna' go see my new friend so he can make me forget my prick husband."

Chapter 6

T.G. pushed the old GMC Jimmy along the highway, hurrying to get out of Milwaukee. Yvette rode next to him. Sir sat in front of her, his chin resting on her leg while she leaned back, staring blankly out of the windshield.

In the back seat, Bucks sat with Julie on his lap. She leaned back against him, comforted by his arms being wrapped around her. Rock lay on the seat next to them, stretched out with his head against Bucks' thigh.

All was silent. T.G. was plagued with tunnel vision. In all his and Bucks' time being in the streets, they had yet to see what they'd just seen in the last twenty-four hours.

Julie's phone rang right then. Bucks grabbed her handbag for her and got her phone out. Julie saw it was Lieutenant Michaels. She told Yvette, then answered the call on speaker mode.

"Tran! What the hell is goin' on?" Michaels barked.

"A lot," she replied.

"No shit! Where's Jones? I've been callin' her phone for the last ten minutes! No answer!"

"She got rid of it, sir. Someone's tracking it, so we had to dump it."

"I'm here, Lieutenant," Yvette spoke out.

"Where are you two at?"

T.G and Bucks' hearts dropped when they heard the lieutenant's question. It was extremely hard for them to remember that the ladies were cops, and even harder for them to wrap their heads around the fact that because they were cops, other dirty or clean cops would be in their lives.

"Heading back to Illinois. I think at this point, it doesn't matter where we go," Julie chimed back in. "People wanna' keep on testin' us? Cool. We gon' ace all of 'em."

"Come to my place. I'll be waiting. Do not have me come looking for you two, Tran and Jones."

"Yes sir," Julie and Yvette answered at the same time.

"Are your boyfriends still with you?" Michaels asked.

"Til the wheels fall off, sir," Bucks spoke out.

"Good to hear. Keep it like that."

Michaels ended the call without a word more.

"Well. Guess we have somewhere to lay our heads for a while," Julie said, tucking her phone back into her bag.

"Somewhere safe too. Michaels is crazy, but his wife... oooweee! Madea would run if Miss Michaels gave her that eye that makes people's bowels loosen," Yvette added.

"We are goin' to a Illinois State Trooper lieutenant's house? How is this in any way a good thing for me and my nigga to do?" T.G. asked, wondering if it sounded crazy to anyone else but him.

Yvette turned her head and looked at him. "Think about it. Would a Colombian shot caller go there looking for you or Bucks? Or other cops? Webster?"

T.G. saw her point right away.

"Okay. You right," he said, fully understanding her logic. "Goin' to yo' boss's crib is like when niggas sell dope at a crib across the street from a police station. No cop would think anybody would be dumb enough to do that."

Yvette chuckled. "No. Nobody would be dumb enough to come to Jarvis Michaels' neck of the woods with ill intentions. His wife is *not* a normal woman."

"Not even close," Julie added for emphasis, knowing the queen of the hood very well.

***

Yvette directed T.G. off the E-way to their destination. He kept his eyes open because he and Bucks knew how Chiraq got down. Stories of street wars out south, out west, east and even up north. When he saw the big Puerto Rican flag on a metal display over the road, he knew instantly where Yvette had him.

He reached Beach and Spaulding soon after. Making a turn, he saw mobs of men and women, hoodied up, no doubt strapped up. A few wore black and gold, some wore fitted and snapbacks to the left.

She pointed to a two-story building on the left where Michaels' department Expedition was parked. T.G. parked two houses up, thinking that parking a stolen vehicle in front of a cop's house, even with cops in it, wasn't the best idea.

They hopped out with the dogs. The second the last door closed, they hear someone shout, "AMOR DE REY!"

T.G. went and took his woman's hand, keeping her close, Bucks did the same with Julie. Sir and Rock stayed close to them as well, ears pricked up, listening for anything sounding like it was getting too close.

A group of five emerged from the gangway between two homes, a couple with Pit Bulls on thick chain leashes.

More came from around the corner at the four-way, with more dogs. Sir and Rock went and stood in front of their humans, ready to go at it.

"Aye, y'all lost or somethin'?" asked a heavy, hoodied up Puerto Rican dude, with filled-in tear drops at the sides of both of his eyes, and a five-point crown tattooed on the left side of his neck, much like the other guys and girls he was accompanied by.

"We just came to visit a friend, my guy," T.G. spoke up, with Yvette at his side and Sir at hers.

"A friend?" the man asked with a puzzled eyebrow. "Ain't no friends around here, Joe. It's King love or no love, fam.

You in my hood, and I don't like it when people I don't know come into my hood."

Bucks stepped up next to his bro, keeping Julie behind him. The two refused to back down, even with more Latin Kings and Queens approaching, coming out from their hiding spots that they all posted in, watching their streets for opps invading their turf.

They eyed the man and those at his side. The man eyed them back. For a minute, they stared at each other, testing each other's gangster for any signs of weakness.

Then suddenly, the big Boricua started chuckling.

T.G. and Bucks got ready to up and start dumping. They knew all too well a death laugh when they heard one.

"Aye, Yvette, JuJu," the guy said to them. "Y'all got cha'll some good dudes here, Joe. Other niggas would've took off runnin' from thirty Spaulding Kings."

T.G. and Bucks both turned around, with shock etched in their faces. They saw the girls smiling slyly. Sir and Rock even seemed to be smiling while they panted with their tongues hanging out the sides of their mouths.

"Yeah, we got us some very loving and passionate men, Oro," Yvette said to the leader of the mob, putting her arm around T.G. and holding him close. "They protect us, and we protect them."

"Until the end of time, big dog," Julie added, holding Bucks' hand.

The girls then introduced Oro's mob to T.G. and Bucks. They were both, once again, amazed that the two lady cops were still so hood. There weren't many cops that could walk through Chicago's infamously dangerous Humboldt Park neighborhood and live to tell about it. When Yvette informed the two that Beach and Spaulding had been their home for most of their childhood, it made sense why they were so welcomed there.

Lieutenant Michaels and his Puerto Rican wife came out of the house Yvette had initially pointed out to T.G. Along with the lieutenant, was his white American Bulldog, with brown brindle patches on his back and his right ear.

"Why y'all botherin' my young ones, Oro?" Michaels' beautiful brown wife with stacked bodacious curves asked, hugging Yvette and Julie. Her hair was tinged with gray, but she had no wrinkles, nor did she seem like a woman in her fifties.

"Testin' their boyfriends out, Mama Queen," Oro replied respectfully, acknowledging her with a hug, then kissing her hand. "You know we can't have scary-ass punks shakin' up with Yvette and JuJu."

"From what I hear," the woman said, casting a glance at T.G. and Bucks. "They are far from punks."

Lieutenant Michael introduced his wife then. Belinda shook their hands, nodding her respect to them. She then dismissed Oro and his goons back to where they were.

"Why that dude call her Mama Queen?" T.G. asked Yvette, as they all followed Michaels, Mama Queen, their dog Damar, into the two-family split house, with three bedrooms in each one.

"Because she's both the queen of Humboldt Park, and to a lot of people, she's mama," Yvette informed him.

***

Immediately, after going to the second-floor apartment, Yvette and T.G. went to shower off all the grime and stress from such a hectic day.

T.G. held her in his arms as streams of hot water pelted them. As they both soaked, Yvette's emotions got the best of her. She burst into tears and sobbed loudly.

He tightened his arms around her, holding her close enough so that she could feel how hard his heart was thumping in his chest. Her cries made his own eyes well up with tears. Together, they both shared the emotional minute. Realization of how things had just gone spiraling out of control had hit them like a bag of bricks. And neither of them would bet anything would get better anytime soon.

***

Bucks sighed. Kneeling next to Julie, he held her hair back, while she puked her guts up into the toilet.

"Bae, yo' ass ain't ate nothin' in hours, so don't tell me you ate somethin' that don't agree with you. You are worried sick…literally."

She lifted her head and looked at him, with red puffy eyes. She felt horrible, and she knew she looked even worse. Bucks couldn't remember ever seeing Julie looking so distraught before. She was the most resilient chick he had ever met.

"I just feel like somethin' really bad is about to happen, Bucks," Julie admitted, hating that feeling with a passion.

"Shit can hit the fan all it wants, JuJu. All that matters when it does is that I'm with you, 'til death do us part, I am *not* leavin' you again, so death can go suck a dirty dick and take someone else."

Julie busted out laughing at him.

"You are too funny, bae. This is why I love you so much."

She twisted her lips up as she laughed.

"Gimme a kiss," she told him.

"Brush yo' teeth first."

"No! Kiss me!"

"Fuck no, nasty, moo-shoo-pork mouth girl."

"Ugh! You get on my fuckin' nerves, Bernard!" Julie said, getting up from the floor, while Bucks stayed where he was, laughing his ass off at her.

***

Later that following afternoon, Yvette, T.G., Julie and Bucks were all awakened by the aromas of meat frying. Sir and Rock were up and posted at the bedroom doors, anxious to be let out.

Getting up from the comfortable beds, the four threw on some clothes and made their way down to the first floor.

Classic Jazz music came from the kitchen, where the delectable smells were coming from. T.G. and Bucks followed the ladies and dogs into the kitchen. Damar hopped up from his plush dog bed by the patio's sliding glass door and ran to greet his two canine guests.

Mama Queen was working the stove. She was cheffing up a big breakfast of country fried steak and eggs, with fried potatoes. Lieutenant Michaels was sitting at the glass dining table, on the phone. They noticed he had a frown on his face. Yvette and Julie couldn't imagine that anything good was being said.

"Join me," he said to them.

"I'll feed the dogs," Mama Queen offered, dumping crispy potatoes onto a plate.

The ladies thanked her. They and their men sat with the lieutenant. Michaels took a deep breath, then exhaled.

"I have no good news… at all," he started with.

The four sighed, muttering curses under their breaths.

"However, there is now light at the end of the tunnels," Michaels continued.

Yvette, Julie, T.G. and Bucks listened as he explained. Mama Queen served them all plates with cups of passion fruit juice. She made herself one and joined, sitting next to her husband.

"When exactly is this supposed to happen?" Julie asked him.

"Today. So, eat, shower and get dressed like it's a day in the office in meetings with important people," Michaels told them. "It is going to be a very long day, week and month."

***

That's crazy," T.G. said, sitting on the bed with Sir laid out next to him. "This is not fair at all."

"Relax," Yvette told him, as she applied burgundy lip gloss to her lips. "We'll be back soon, then we can go out to eat or somethin'."

"I'm not talkin' about you havin' to leave. I'm talkin' 'bout you wearin' that and refusin' to lemme' hit that from the back before you go?"

Yvette was looking like a professional trend setter in her enticing outfit. Her hair was spiral curled and left to hang loose, pearls were in her ears, and around her neck. She had chosen a burgundy form-fitting leather Saint Laurent dress with a pleated mid-thigh hem, long sheer lace sleeves, and a low-cleavage breast line.

T.G. felt his dick hardening in his pants. He just could not get over how beautiful she was in a T-shirt and jeans, but when she was glammed up, whether for professional reasons or to go out, he yearned for her.

His eyes rolled downwards to her thick thighs, taking in the black pantyhose with YSL woven all over them, and the burgundy suede knee-high stiletto boots she had on. She had him fiending for her like a dope head fresh out of a two-day stay at a county jail. Instant visuals of him bending her over and fucking her hard from the back filled his mind to the point he came close to having a wet dream while he was still awake.

***

Yvette turned around and saw the way T.G. was gazing at her. It made her feel so sexy.

"You lookin' at me like you got a problem, my man," she told him, taking seductive steps towards him, until she was right in front of him.

"I do! I'm tryna' fuck, and you keepin' my pussy from me, wit' cho' stingy ass!"

Yvette started laughing at the salty look on his face. She took his hands and pulled him up from the bed. Without any words, she reached down to his crotch and started undoing his pants.

"Eeeeeee! I know you couldn't resist this dick, baby! Gon' 'n let a nigga beat it up from the back!"

"Negative, I ain't got no time for all that," she told him, pulling his cock out, felling it pulsate in her hand. "But if you'll shut cho' ass up for a minute, I'ma suck on this dick real good before I go."

T.G. shut it up and watched her sink down to her knees. She put her sexy lips to the bulbous tip and kissed it, before she licked around it. T.G.'s eyes rolled to the back of his head when she opened wide and engulfed him, balls deep. He groaned and cursed, powerless to her unbelievable oral skills. And Yvette loved it.

***

"Ooooooo, Bernard! Oohh, my God! Shit! Eaah! Oooo!"

Julie cried out in ecstasy. Between her legs, Bucks sucked on her clit like a pussy-eating monster. He was unable to help but snatch her up, toss her on the bed, and dive in between her legs like an Olympic swimmer when the Vietnamese beauty came out of the bathroom, wearing a chocolate Burberry long-sleeved top, with a low cleavage line, a beige, brown and green plaid Burberry skirt, with chocolate-colored pantyhose and beige pointed-toe Jimmy Choo pumps.

Her hair was pulled up into a tight bun that looked like a flower bud on the top of her head. Her bangs encircled her face. Black eyeliner, and red lip gloss was the only makeup she put on. The gold Tiffany & Co necklace that Bucks had bought her, with the gold watch to match, was around her neck and flicking on her wrist.

He had to have her. She looked beyond delicious when she wore such sophisticated office-like attire.

He had rushed her, put her up against the wall, kissed her wildly, heating her up. His hunger for her set her on fire. She could reach an orgasm just off his desire for her.

Bucks then took Julie to the bed, laid her down and as he continued to kiss her, he pushed her skirt up. Her pantyhose came down, then her red lace panties with his name embroidered into the crotch. He pulled them down to her ankles, put her legs all the way up, then licking his lips at it, Bucks dove in headfirst like he thought he was Michael Phelps.

***

The music from his iPhone synched to the wireless Bluetooth speakers played. Lil' Durk and Jeremih's "Like Me" was on. Bucks sucked and slurped Julie up like she was a cone of melting ice cream, not wanting a single drop of her sweet sugar to go to waste.

Julie's legs were up high. Her hands caressed her own breasts. She bit her bottom lip, moaning, back arching, as Bucks pleasured her like he would never get to do it again.

Minutes later, Julie's whole body started shaking, trembling like she was a washing machine on spin cycle that wasn't bolted down. Bucks could tell she was seconds away. He took her the rest of the way there and drank her up when she exploded.

Julie went limp on the bed. Depleted of energy and air, she lay there, breathing hard and fast.

Bucks pulled her panties and pantyhose back up, then crawled up next to her. Julie turned and looked into his eyes. He gazed into hers. Love was there, fire and desire, passion and understanding.

"You drive me crazy," she told him, with a smile radiating how infatuated she was with him.

"So? You ain't gon' do shit about it, punk," he replied back, with the smile that always made her heart beat like an early Twista song.

She scooted in and kissed his wet lips. "You can think that all you want, Bernard, but just wait 'til I get back, punk. Your ass is all mine, baby."

Chapter 7

Yvette and Julie met up with Lieutenant Michaels at the front door. He was dressed in a Lacoste polo shirt, slacks and leather dress shoes. His service weapon was strapped inside his holster, with his badge clipped to his belt.

His wife came and gave him a loving kiss on the lips, then hugged Yvette and Julie. They left the house, making their way to the lieutenant's personal vehicle. They hopped inside Michaels' gray and black 2022 GMC Yukon XL. Michaels pulled out of the spot and got on the way to where their meeting was to take place.

***

A short while later, Michaels entered a tall circular parking structure that sat off to the side of the Chicago River, close to Michigan Avenue. Yvette, sitting up front, surveyed the area. Cars, SUVs, pick-ups new and old littered the parking spaces. Every bend they turned, more spaces filled.

Michaels came to where a silver two-door BMW coupe was sitting parked behind a row of cars that were actually parked. Yvette and Julie immediately zeroed in on it. The windshield was tinted, and so were the other windows. Neither of them could see who was inside.

He pulled up in front of the car, parking nose up to the M3. He cut the engine and took a deep breath, before exhaling.

"Uh… Lieutenant? Is everything okay?" Yvette asked, with a bad feeling in her gut.

Julie was wondering the same thing.

Michaels looked at Yvette. "No. Everything isn't alright, Jones. Hopefully though, these people can change that for us. Come on," he said, and got out of the SUV.

Yvette glanced back at her bestie, her lover, her friend. Julie looked at her. They exchanged no words at the moment. They both got out with their handbags, loaded with their semi-automatics.

***

"What up, fam? The hell y'all niggas been doin', Joe? We hearin' a whole lot of shit over here, my nigga!" said Flip, sounding very bothered.

Out in the backyard of Michaels' house, T.G. and Bucks were sitting at a table on the small porch, while Sir, Rock and Damar ran around in the brisk coolness of the dwindling summer.

They were talking amongst themselves, attempting to put their own strategy for survival together. Bucks suggested they keep it hood and call the guys, so T.G. hit up Flip, who was with Low and GB, three certified goons that they both trusted with their lives.

"That's because a whole lotta shit been goin' down, bruh," T.G. said, speaking out so his homies could hear him and Bucks on speaker mode.

"Aight, so what chu' need us to do? We ready, my nigga," he and Bucks heard Low say just then.

"We gotta stay tucked for a minute. A crooked white boy on one wit' us and our girls, you dig what I'm sayin'?" T.G. asked.

He heard one of them curse, which meant at least one of them understood that there was cop trouble.

"Man, fuck twelve, Joe! They bleed like us!" G.B. suddenly swapped. "On my momma, fam! We can go dump on all they asses! I been ready since they did that to that brotha' up in Minnesota! And lil momma in Kentucky! All my people that them bitch ass cops killed! On God!"

"Bro, calm down a little bit," T.G told him. "The situation is a little bit more... delicate than that."

In so many words, T.G. explained. He told the guys who their women were, the drama going on with them, and where they were.

Listening to it, Bucks was mystified about how they were really in this situation.

This is like some movie shit. Two dope boys and they girls bein' hunted by dirty white cops, and Colombian hitters... who will win? he thought, then inside his head he added, *us!*

"Aye, bro," Bucks spoke up then, after the perfect person to lend a hand popped into his head.

T.G. turned his head and looked at him.

"You remember ol' boy we met a couple years ago? That Dominican dude, with the long braids and green eyes?" Bucks asked.

Instant recognition of who his homeboy spoke about registered in his mind. His eyes went wide as he realized why Bucks was bringing the man up.

"Who Bucks talkin' about, Joe?" they both heard Flip ask.

"The answer to all our problems. Famo," T.G. replied. "Stand by my niggas, we gon' get back at y'all in a minute."

"We here, Joe," Flip said, then ended the call.

T.G. looked at his guy. "We don't got his number, bro."

Bucks nodded. "True, but we can still slide on him."

"How?"

Bucks pulled his phone out and went into his Lyft app, ordering a ride.

"We gon' pull up," he then said, looking at T.G.

"Nigga, we can't just pull up on a made man like that! Dude is Dominican mafia, bro! Are you outta yo' muthafuckin' mind?"

Bucks looked at him. "Gotta better idea?"

T.G. shook his head. "Naw," he sighed. "Fuck it. Let's let the lady of the house know we steppin' out."

***

An Hour Later...

Back in Michaels' SUV, Yvette and Julie were both dumbfounded. The manila folders in their hands filled with paperwork were proof that the meeting had not been a figment of their imagination. Between the two women they had met, the things they wanted, Michaels seeming to be for it, and the ultimatum that came at the very end, they both felt overwhelmed with grief.

"I know it's a lot to take in," Michaels spoke as he headed around to a restaurant with outdoor dining. "Just keep in mind what's at risk if we fail. Sikes has already been issued his tasks."

Yvette sighed to herself. She was at a loss for words.

Julie was silent as well. Looking out of the window as Michaels slow rolled behind a CTA bus, she found herself wishing that she could snap her fingers, and it would all be over.

"You two are the closest things to daughters that I've ever had," continued Michaels. "I will not let anything happen to you."

Julie's phone rang. She got it out of her handbag and saw Bucks was calling. A smile instantly came to her face.

"Hey handsome," she answered, wishing so badly that he was with her right then.

"Hey, baby. Where you at?"

Julie saw they were parking in a spot in front of a pizza spot.

"The city, about to get some pizza. You?"

"Enroute to go make a move that 's either gonna help us out in the greatest way or do absolutely nothin' for us," Bucks told her.

"Um… care to elaborate?"

Michaels cut the engine off. They all opened their doors to get out. Bucks ran down his plan to Julie as she followed Yvette and Michaels into the restaurant.

"You know them?" Julie asked with shock.

"No, chance meeting."

Stopping where she was, Julie's eyebrows furrowed.

"Sooo… What in God's name makes you think someone that high up will join forces and step in?"

"Real niggas recognize other real niggas. Our reputations don't ring bells anywhere near as loud as dude's and his family's, but I bet money, our names dun' been heard by them."

Julie stepped in line with Yvette and Michaels, ready to order.

"Okay, Bernard. Just be careful. Call me if you need me, baby."

"I will. Your stomach feelin' better?" Bucks tossed in.

"Haven't thought about it, but it must be, I haven't been throwin' up lately."

"Aight, bae. Love you," Bucks told her.

"I love you too, Bernard. See you when you get back. Remember what I said, too."

Bucks laughed. "I will never forget that, gorgeous."

***

Bucks ended the call with a smile on his face. He sat back in the seat of the Lyft driver's Prius, wishing Julie was with him right at that moment.

In the seat next to him, T.G. was back on the phone with Flip.

"I'ma make it happen, Joe," T.G. replied to what Flip had just told him.

"Please do. Them niggas got that Kill Bill, fam. We needs that. The re-up stash is ready too."

"Say less. I'ma get at you in a few," T.G. said, then he ended the call.

The Lyft driver was just turning off the highway onto Wadsworth Road to head west. T.G. and Bucks chatted amongst themselves. Ten minutes later, their destination came up on the right, at the corner of Wadsworth and Green Bay Road.

The whole intersection teemed with businesses with the name Valdez on them. Across from where they were going was a big semi-truck and trailer dealership, with a big garage that a few very fancy semis sat in front of, looking worthy of being in top-notch car and truck shows, and even rap music videos.

Opposite from the dealership and customizing shop, was a car customizing business, with a few ol' schools on big rims, a few rare edition foreigners, and some exotic cars.

A big gas station with a truck stop behind it was across from the car shop. At the corner where T.G. and Bucks were turning into was a high-end jewelry store.

Valdez Fine Jewelry & Diamond Co. was painted on the windowless entrance door. There were no windows at all. The lot was nearly filled with cars and SUVs that cost as much as the diamond jewelry inside.

***

Posted out front, a trio of men that were as wide and big as refrigerators, with long braids and tattoos on their faces stood by a gleaming, emerald-green Lamborghini Aventador LP 770 Superveloce.

The Lyft driver pulled up to the front. T.G. and Bucks quickly hopped out. They marched towards the front door and drew looks from the men.

"Y'all got an appointment?" one of them asked, as all three stood their enormous sumo-wrestler frames in front of the door, with their hands by their waistlines.

T.G. and Bucks stood their ground. They showed no fear. The pistols they had gave them a sense of security, but still they knew they were in uncharted waters, and did not want to make waves.

"Naw, fam. We just came to see if we might be able to speak with Javier," Bucks told the man.

The three looked at each other, then back at T.G. and Bucks. At least, T.G. and Bucks thought they were looking at them.

"Search 'em," one of the other giants said.

T.G. and Bucks suddenly felt hands grab them from behind, holding them in place. They struggled to get free out of survival instinct. Two more huge men appeared and patted them down. Right away, they found T.G.'s and Bucks pistols and relieved them of their weapons.

"Come to speak with cannons?" one of the men asked.

"Bro, we are always strapped. We know how niggas get down in this family," Bucks said. "You think if we was comin' for his head, that we would walk into the lion's den with a fork?"

T.G. and Bucks heard one laugh. It wasn't coming from any of the security.

"That's a good one, homie. I haven't heard that before," they heard.

A tall muscular man with deep cocoa-complexioned skin stepped in front of them. He was sporting a Balenciaga fit, diamond jewelry, Timberlands, and a fresh bald-fade hair cut with the curls-for-the-girls on top. His beard was so sharply lined that it looked painted on.

"So, y'all wanna see the man with the green eyes, huh?" he asked them, giving them both the same amount of eye contact.

"Yes," Bucks replied, not faltering at all. "We could really use his help, man. I met him a while back. He may or may not remember me, but me and my guy come in peace."

"With guns," the man added.

Bucks and T.G. looked at him.

"Would you go somewhere unfamiliar without protection?" T.G. asked, finally speaking up.

The man chuckled. "No motherfuckin' way. Follow me, I'll take you to see that green-eyed nigga. Hopefully, he ain't in a bad mood from your pop-up visit."

***

Bucks followed the man into the building. T.G. followed him, not liking having had his gun taken like a child's toy be taken away.

Inside, plenty of people were shopping around gazing at the exclusive custom designed pieces of jewelry. Everything inside the glass display cases shined so hard that it was like they were made of light themselves.

Security was everywhere. There would be no smash-n-grab there, Bucks could see.

The man led them past all the shoppers, to the rear where a short and incredibly gorgeous brown-sugar complexioned woman stood, assisting another woman with a vintage Rolex.

Bucks and T.G. were flabbergasted by the short chick. Her hair was streaked with gold, infused with natural dark silky roots, pulled tightly up into a sophisticated bun on the top of her head. Her baby hair edges gelled around her stunning model-like face. Diamond earrings dangled from her ears, with a diamond choker chain around her neck. She wore a tight red dress with brown snakeskin trim, and stilettos that matched the trim. Her wrists and fingers were iced out with flawless diamonds. She looked like a queen, one that commanded respect without having to say a word.

The woman smiled at the man that had led them to her.

"Un memento, senora," she said to her customer, then to the man, "Quien son ellos?"

The guy responded, "Quieren hablar con tu esposo. Dicen que necesitan su ayuda."

The woman then looked at Bucks and T.G., who were lost by the Spanish being spoken by the woman, but also by the man, who they definitely thought was Black.

"Nice to meet y'all," the lady then said, with what sounded like a New York accent to Bucks and T.G. "I'm Michelle, and this is my brother-in-law, Xavier. My husband is in the back room. Give me a minute to finish with this customer, and I'll take you to see him."

"Thank you, ma'am," Bucks replied with a head nod.

Xavier walked off then, leaving Bucks and T.G. waiting. After Michelle finished with her client, she told them to follow her.

They trailed her, trying so hard to keep their eyes off her big round plump ass cheeks. The way the bounce with every step she took enticed Bucks and T.G., making them both feel super guilty to be ogling the ass of a woman whose husband they desired help from.

***

She led them out of the showroom floor, through a long hallway, to a big glossy oak door.

Michelle opened the door and stood to the side, gesturing for Bucks and T.G. to enter.

They stepped inside the sleek presidential-designed office and first saw the two demonic-looking dogs, standing next to the big mahogany desk. They looked like big Pit Bulls, both of them were black with brown brindle patterns, clipped ears, with tall muscular bodies. Neither of them growled, nor looked ready to attack, but then again, neither did Sir or Rock before they were commanded to kill.

Behind the desk, was the man of the hour. His green eyes were focused right on Bucks and T.G.

His hair was braided in fresh Iverson, tails hanging down past his chest. He wore a black tank top. Two long white gold diamond chains hung around his neck, flickering hard. His muscular shoulder, chest, and his tatted-up arms were on full display.

Bucks couldn't help but think how the golden-brown toned Dominican resembled a thuggish Colin Kaepernick, with diamond studs in his ears.

"Papi, estos hombres les gustaria hablar contigo," Michelle told him, then she stepped out, closing the door behind her.

"How's it goin', Bucks? T.G.?" he asked, standing his five foot eleven tall athletic frame up.

Bucks and T.G. both furrowed their brows. The man knew their names. Bucks had run into the guy when he was solo and had never introduced himself.

T.G. was puzzled as well, but in the back of his mind, he was very sure that a man with a background like his, likely knew everything about everyone that came within ten feet of him.

Bucks' eyes glanced down at the two Cane Corsos, both who were still standing guard, staring at him and his guy.

"Don't worry about them, my dude. They won't even growl unless me or my wife says so," he told Bucks. "I'm sure you already know my name, so tell me what it is you seek assistance on?"

Javier Omar Valdez invited the two to sit.

"Demon, Diamond. Relajanse," Javi told the trained killers.

They obeyed his command and sat down, but still kept their eyes on Bucks and T.G.

They both sat in the two chairs in front of Javi's desk.

"If I may," said Javi, right before Bucks could speak. "I already know why you're here. My question is, what makes you think I can help you out?" Javi looked at Bucks. "I can't even understand why you haven't gone to Mexico or Japan, all them people you're accused of knockin' off." He looked at T.G. "and you, yo woman is highly coveted by that clown ass cop, who has enough years on the force and experience, to get you up outta the way… for good."

"With all due respect, Javi," Bucks said feeling his heart rate increasing every second. "We know who runs this whole region, niggas bow to y'all, the law fears y'all. Meetin' you that day at the little fry-shack spot in Waukegan, I knew who you was. Yo' face, yo' peoples' faces, been on the news more than Donald Trump's bitch ass, after he got shot with what we all know was a fuckin' paintball."

Javi busted out laughing. "I said the same thing, Joe! Fuck that punk-ass cracker! Kamala Harris for Pres, goddammit!"

"Agreed," T.G. said.

Javi looked at them again. For a minute he sat silently. Bucks and T. G. wondered what was going through the man's mind.

He pulled out his iPhone a second later and made a call. Bucks and T.G. sat and waited as Javi started speaking in Spanish to whoever answered.

"Oye, tigueraso. Yo tengo los tipos que los puercos buscan. Necisitan ayuda. Que dice, primo?"

Not understanding a single word, Bucks and his homie prayed to God that Javi wasn't calling in a hit squad, while they just sat there.

"Fa' sho," Javi said, then ended the call.

He looked at them. "My cousin wants to meet you. Let's ride."

"Like… right now?" Bucks asked as Javi stood up.

"Naw, when the cops catch you and give you the street death penalty," Javi replied sarcastically. "Come on, man. If y'all seek help from a nigga like me, y'all muhfuckas gon' have to be quick and on yo' toes. Vamos!"

Chapter 8

"I can help with that… Sounds like fun."

Julie and Yvette both smirked at the response on Yvette's iPhone. At the pizza spot, Julie had come up with a suggestion to have their own plan of attack that neither Webster nor Reuben would ever see coming.

"The Problem Solver is on board, biatch!" Julie exclaimed, geeked to have a straight monster on the team.

"This is gonna even out the odds significantly!" Yvette said, replying to the message with, *You are literally a life saver, E! I'll keep you posted.*

She put her phone up and looked at Michaels. He was staring at them both, curious as hell as to what they were up to,

"Y'all look like cats that ate the baby birds," he told them.

Yvette and Julie laughed at him.

"Well," said Yvette. "When you really think about all the resources you have that can, and will give all that oppose a real fight, it gives a girl like me a big smile, sir."

"As long as these so-called resources don't bring more trouble, then I'm for it," he said.

"Oh, trust and believe," Julie chimed in. "This guy will bring a lot of trouble, but not in our direction, boss man."

Yvette and Julie high-fived each other, then shouted, "Problem solved, biiiatch!"

***

Miky Woodz's "No Le Baje (Como En Los Viejos Tiempos,)" pounded from the back of Javi's dark-red Mercedes G63 AMG as he pushed west on Route 173. Riding shotgun, Bucks nodded his head to the Puerto Rican rapper's song. He couldn't understand a damn thing being said, but the shit pounded so hard from the subwoofers.

T.G. sat in the rear row, hoping that whatever was to come of the trip, he might be able to gain a connect on the most coveted cocaine to hit the United States, next to Pablo Escobar's.

Far past any towns in Lake County, Javi rode along a long desolate two-way road, out in the farm and country sections of Belvidere, Illinois. After he passed a large oak tree stump on his right, he slowed down and came to a gravel driveway.

Javi turned and headed up the path-road. Almost a mile back from the road, the massive city-sized chemical producing plant came into view. Bucks' eyes went wide when he saw it. T.G. looked through the middle of the SUV, out of the windshield, seeing the gigantic plant, surrounded by tall chain-link fencing, topped by barbwire.

At the secured entrance, Javi rolled right through when the gate slid open. He pushed through the busy plant, being waved and honked at by so many employees and truck drivers that Bucks and T.G. thought the green-eyed Taino owned the place.

Minutes later, Javi pulled up to a colossal building, with what looked like two garage doors, big enough for a cruise ship to fit through.

A row of exotic and luxury cars were parked in front. Bucks saw a huge muscular man get out of the passenger's seat of a baby blue and black Jean-Pierre Wimille edition Bugatti Veyron Roadster. From the driver's seat, an amazingly gorgeous Amazon tall woman got out.

The man sported a clean bald-fade haircut and a neat beard, with diamonds in his ears, in the two Cuban link chains around his neck, and on his wrist, an outrageously expensive Roger Dubuis X Lamborghini Excaliber Spider Camtech watch. Despite all his pricey drip, he wore just a black thermal top, black 501's, and black Air Yeezy 1's.

The stunning beauty had long silky hair that was as sapphire blue as the one-point-five-million-dollar Jacob & Co X Bugatti Tourbillion on her wrist. She was a few shades lighter than the caramel-skinned giant. She was dressed in a black denim bodysuit with her Air Yeezies on her feet, and blue lip gloss on. What Bucks and T.G. noticed right away as Javi led them over to the two was the woman's frosty arctic blue eyes that matched the big blue diamond ring on her finger.

"Bucks and T.G., this my cousin Danny, and his wife Ximena, 'erybody calls her ChaCha," Javi introduced.

"Good to meet y'all," Bucks said, shaking hands with the two, who had the presence of true royalty if he never felt it before.

T.G. shook their hands next.

"We been hearin' a whole lot about y'all, yo," ChaCha said, with a New York accent. "Y'all niggaz is crazy, B. All them fiends, and a muthafuckin' cop, though?" she said, looking right at Bucks with her piercing eyes.

He shrugged, not willing to admit to anything, though he knew that telling them wouldn't leave their lips. He and T.G. had heard of Daniel Valdez, and his wife. Pablo and Griselda would get very jealous of the Dominican cocaine overlord, and his Colombian and Puerto Rican mixed queen pin wife.

"It's all good, home boy," Danny then spoke, in a smooth baritone voice. "It ain't like we all ain't had to do some crazy things to make it up out of a jam. I respect y'all's survival instincts. My little cuz here tells me y'all would like a hand in dealin' with ya troubles. Your ladies are cops, they helpin' out too or what?"

"Of course they are," T. G. cut in, taking offense to it sounding like his woman was being questioned.

"Oye, papa, relax," ChaCha said to him, sensing the quick flash. "We know Yvette and JuJu are on the 'bizness. Between the two of them and us, we have a mutual friend that they've called in to help as well."

Bucks and T.G. exchanged glances with each other.

"Who?" T.G. asked her.

"He's known as the Problem Solver," Danny told him.

"Check it out," ChaCha spoke again. "We will help you out, that's word to motha, son, but my husband and I need a little help ourselves. Follow us."

Entering the building, Bucks and T.G. followed Danny and ChaCha, with Javi bringing up the rear.

Men and women in different uniforms hustled around the facility, performing important tasks to keep Valdez Chemical, Inc. functioning twenty-four-seven, three-sixty-five. They ended up in the big garage minutes later. Inside, a glossy Kenworth W990, and a glossy Peterbilt 389, both black, decked out with a lot of chrome and gigantic exhaust pipes. They were both coupled to fifty-three-foot-long dry van box trailers.

Behind the Peterbilt was a blacked-out Chevy Avalanche.

"So," ChaCha said, turning towards Bucks and T.G. "To answer the questions that are swimming around in your heads, we're all taking a little trip. My husband and I need to deliver the loads inside of these trailers to some people… ASAP."

"Uh… okay," said Bucks, with a little hesitation. "I don't know how to drive an eighteen-wheeler, though."

"Neither do I," T.G. said, looking at the massive semi-trucks.

Danny, ChaCha and Javi busted out laughing. Bucks looked at his homie, puzzled as to what was so funny.

"It's all good, you. We'll drive them," ChaCha said, pulling out the keys to her Peterbilt.

Danny pulled the keys to his Kenworth out. "You both ride with Javi in the Avalanche and follow us down. We got a long ride ahead of us, so y'all gon' need to rotate drivers."

"Sheeeit, not me. I'm a driver, nigga," Javi said to his big cousin, with the keys to the Chevy in his hand. "I hope neither one of y'all like doin' the speed limit drivin' like an ol' lady," he said to Bucks and T.G. with a grin.

T.G. chuckled, "This nigga drive like an ol' lady without feet and hands."

The three busted out laughing. Bucks waved them off.

"Yo momma drive like an ol' lady without feet and hands," he shot back.

ChaCha, Danny and Javi all laughed harder.

"Yoooo, he sounds just like Macho wit' that 'yo momma' shit, bae!" she said to her husband.

"Macho?" Bucks questioned.

"My other little cousin. You'll meet him and his older brother very soon," Danny said. "But for now, we gotta head out. Call 'ya ladies 'n tell 'em y'all be back in a few days."

"A few days?" T.G. asked in shock.

"We ain't goin' around the block, player," ChaCha said as the door they had come through opened up, and two groups of scientists carrying two gigantic wooden crates on wooden beam poles entered, heading towards the semi's trailers.

Each trailer got a crate. They were secured inside, the doors to the trailers were closed and locked, then the groups went back to the lab without uttering a single word.

"Alrighty, people," ChaCha said, pointing her remote starter at her truck and starting the engine, as Danny remote started his truck's engine. "Let's hit the road. Next stop... M-I-YAYO!"

Bucks and T.G. both gasped.

"Miami?" Bucks questioned, tripping hard.

Javi patted his shoulder. "Don't trip, my nigga. Expect the unexpected. You, yo' homeboy and y'all's mujeres gon' be aight. Let's get up outta here 'n get it done." The billionaire

Dominican climbed up into his KW, and his billionaire wife hopped up into her Pete.

"Okay, fuck it," Bucks replied.

Without questioning anything further, her and T.G. and Javi hopped into the Avalanche. Bucks started the engine, put it in drive and pulled off behind the two semis, wondering what the hell he had gotten himself and T.G. into.

***

"Are you for real, man?" Yvette asked, exasperated when T.G. told her that he wasn't coming back for a few days.

She heard him sigh.

"Yeah. I have absolutely no clue what we on, but bro got faith in this, I'm ridin' wit' my nigga till the wheels fall off."

Yvette smiled at that. One of the things she truly admired about her dude was how down to ride for his brother from another mother he was, and how real and loyal he was. There was nothing fake about him.

"I understand," she replied as Sir licked her face. "Just be careful. I hear a lot of shit about them people, Tremaine. Them niggas are wild as hell."

T.G. laughed. "Sheeeiit, you tellin' me? Naw, we gon' be aight, though. Gotta give to get, 'ya dig I'm sayin'?"

"Yeah. My only worry is what the hell they request you to give, in order to get."

"To be determined very soon," T.G. told her. "Love you, bae."

"I love you too, baby. Hurry back."

"Yup."

The call ended.

Yvette pulled her dog closer to her and kissed his nose. He licked her face again, returning her love.

Julie walked in seconds later, with Rock and Damar. She was freshly showered and dressed to impress in a tight black, long-sleeved backless dress, covered in gold designs that

Versace so famously used, with black fishnet pantyhose, and gold ankle-strapped Versace stiletto pumps. Her hair was pulled back into a bun, gold Versace glasses rested up above her forehead, and she was draped in gold jewelry.

"You ready?" she asked Yvette, making her way to her, stopping right in front of her.

Yvette felt her panties getting wet at the sight of the Asian beauty. Her body was cold. The dress she had on had her looking like a delicious snack.

She was killing it in the lava-red leather YSL mini dress, with no shoulders, and a slit up the left thigh-high hem. Red fishnet pantyhose accentuated her already delicious-looking legs. On her feet, Yvette rocked leather YSL stiletto pumps.

Yvette and Julie looked good! Their dick-teasingly sexy ensembles were more than necessary for what they had to do.

Yvette stood up. Ignoring Julie's question, she pulled Julie to her by her perky ass, and started kissing her, with a lot of tongue.

She squeezed and gripped Julie's booty, while Julie squeezed and smacked on hers. The two moaned, pussies dripping wet, soaking their panties. They heated each other up, ready to strip naked and go crazy.

Yvette pulled back a second later, finding the strength to do so.

"Yes. I'm ready to get back to normal life," she told her.

Julie chuckled. "Normal life? What's that?"

"It's when the threat of a cop that has plenty of ways to get you buried dies," they suddenly heard their lieutenant say.

Quickly turning towards the doorway, they saw him, dressed in his own get-up for the job. The deep purple tuxedo he had on had a green silk shirt, green gators and a purple fedora with a green feather. His gold Cartier shades had green tinted lenses, around his neck were two thick gold chains, shining like the gold Cartier on his wrist, and the gold rings on his fingers.

Yvette and Julie busted out laughing at how he looked. Michaels stared at them, not even close to smiling.

"Oh, shit! You look like Ving Rhames when he played Melvin on *Baby Boy!*" Yvette clowned, thinking of when the actor's character first appeared in the hit hood flick, puffing on a cigar in the living room of Jody's mother's house.

Michaels shook his head as tears rolled down their eyes.

"I told you, you look crazy, Jarvis!" they all heard Mama Queen shout.

"We got work to do. Bring y'all asses on," Michaels told the two sexy ladies.

They kissed their dogs, gave Damar a peck on his nose, then walking towards Michaels, they started laughing again as they passed by him.

"I'ma kick both y'all's asses," he said, following behind them, heading to leave out and get to the secret auction their new "bosses" managed to get them into.

***

"Bag Of Money," by Rick Ross, Wale, Meek Mill, and T-Pain blared from the speakers around the luxurious presidential suite out in Skokie, Illinois, next to the Old Orchard Mall. Inside, men and women with substantial wealth were dressed in designer clothing, and jewelry. Many of them were sipping expensive aged wines and champagne, while others were partaking in rich-man drugs.

Scantily clad women walked around with bottles on silver trays, making sure no flutes or glasses ever got empty, and trays with mounds of cocaine and clean tooters.

Maurice, a tall hefty man in a gaudy-looking money-green suit, joined by three beautiful women, one Black with ebony skin, one Latina with caramel skin, and an Asian, with a fair-skin tone, all in tiny dresses and heels, made up like runway models, moseyed around, mingling with the wealthy elite guests that had come from all over the country, seeking what he was auctioning off.

Moving from couple, to trio, to quad, Maurice was feeling like he was the man from all the love he was getting, and all the money he would be receiving.

"Aye, man! When's the show gon' start, my dude?" an ol' school cat in a pimp suit, under a long fur coat asked him.

Maurice saw the two gorgeous women he was with. One was in a sexy black and gold dress. She was Asian, something Maurice had always had a fetish for. The second one was a beautiful Black woman, wearing a hot red dress that had him wanting to take her and the Asian chick from the played-out pimp, and add the two vixens to his stable.

"Who are you?" Maurice asked, seeing the man's Cartier frames and Cartier watch, which told him the guy might have a few dollars to spend.

"Oh, my bad, player. They call me Jazz G Funk," the man said.

The two women busted out laughing.

"Somethin' funny?" he snapped on them.

They both shut up right away.

"That's what I thought. Neither one of you bet' not say shit, nor laugh at nothin' else, or I will slap the veneers that I paid fo' outta y'all's mouths! Nod if you understand me!"

Maurice saw the ladies obey him. He smirked, liking when he saw women getting put in their place.

"Sorry about that, my man. Bitches don't know how to act when you try to hold off on slappin' 'em up, 'ya dig I'm sayin'?"

"I do," Maurice nodded. "These ones at my side took a while to break, after I brought 'em to my stable, fresh up outta high school."

"Pimp on, player!" the guy said, giving Maurice props. "Ain't nothin' better than a young bitch that ain't no nigga ran up in yet. I prefer to rope 'em in before they can legally drive. You see, a bitch that's fourteen or fifteen, they do whatever I want 'em to, 'cause they easy to woo. I gets 'em in love with me, then they do what I want. I dun' had these two pretty hoes since they were fifteen and two years later, the dun' already got me ridin' in a Bentley Coupe."

"Good pussy will get that for any pimp that knows how to market his stock," Maurice said.

"Chu'ch! That's why I'm hea', my brotha'. My guy Linx from out the Holy City told me, if I wanna' get into the big leagues, I gots to step my game up."

"You know Linx?" Maurice asked, going wide eyed.

"Oh yeah! Yeah! That's my guy! Me and Linx go waay back to when he had that gold Fleetwood on baskets and vogues!"

"Oooohhh, damn! Aye, man that car was the shit! You know I bought it off him, right?" Maurice said.

"And that 'thang lookin' brand new in the parkin' lot!"

Maurice chuckled, then he looked at the guy once more. He knew Linx, his old running partner. He and Linx used to sell a lot of pussy and heroin back in the 8eighties and nineties. His mans retired from the game in the early 2000s, rich as a bitch. Maurice, now in his late fifties, had no plans to retire. For however long money would be paid by people wanting high class pussy, he was selling it.

"Alright, Jazz G Funk. The show is gon' start in about ten minutes, but that show's for these chumps out here that can't work a young bitch like folks like ourselves. The real show, is in another suite."

"Well, lead the way, my brother." The man dug in his pockets and pulled out four knots of rolled up C-notes. "And this is just what I got in cash. My hoes got more loot in their bags, and I got a Black card in my wallet. Chu'ch!"

Maurice nodded. "Chu'ch! Come on 'n follow me. I'll take you to what you want, my guy."

Maurice and his ladies let the man and his ladies out of the Presidential Suite, up to the top floor, to a penthouse suite. The second they stepped in, Maurice turned to see the looks on their faces when they saw the orgies taking place, all over the wide open-concept main floor.

"Oh… wow," he heard the man say, as his eyes and the two women looked at the young naked girls pleasing anywhere from two to three men, at the same time.

Maurice reached out a hand and touched his guest's shoulder.

"Any time you want, you can go on 'n take yo' pick, Jazz G. I got black, I got white, I got yellow, and I got brown, all flavors for you to savor."

The man nodded his head. "You know what I'd like, my brotha'?"

"Tell me, and I'll make it happen. A friend of Linx's, is a friend of mines."

"I want for every single sick muthafucka like you to die!"

Maurice's eyes went wide in shock when the man opened his coat and pulled out two big Desert Eagle .40s, pointed right at him.

BOOM!

Lieutenant Michaels blew both of his huge cannons at Maurice. A millisecond before it, Maurice dove to the floor, narrowly missing bullets to the face. He rolled away and hopped up, using the pandemonium to his advantage.

The Latina he had with him quickly got a butterfly knife from the strap on her inner thigh, concealed by her dress. While the other two ran, she lunged at Michaels, screaming like a maniac.

WHAM!

Julie smacked the girl with her handbag, which had her Sig Sauer in it. Yvette pulled out her own 9mm while Michaels ran to catch Maurice.

BOC! BOC! BOC! BOC! BOC! BOC!

Yvette and Julie ducked as gunshots rang out. They were just able to catch a glimpse of the security guard up on the upper loft floor, leaning over the balcony, firing a semi-automatic AR-15 at them.

The stakes were high. Bullets had no names. There were a lot of kids inside. Screaming and panicking mixed in with the shooting. Yvette and Julie got into cop mode.

Julie yelled for Yvette to cover her. Yvette held her hand up over the drink counter they were ducked behind and fired. Julie tucked and rolled as the bullets from Yvette's cannon made the guard back up.

She hopped up like an acrobat when she was under the loft. Yvette stopped firing once Julie was clear. She heard crying coming from close by. On her hands and knees with her guns, she crawled, staying low, towards the sound.

Around the corner of the counter, three young girls, as bare as they day they were born, sat against it, taking cover.

"Hey! It's okay! I'm a cop! You're all safe!" she told them.

CLICK CLACK!

Yvette's heart dropped when she felt the barrel of a gun touch the top of her head. Glancing to her right, she saw the hairy legs of a white man.

BOC! BOC! BOC! BOC!

Yvette shrieked, thinking he had fired, until the man dropped dead to the floor right next to her, with two holes in the side of his forehead, and his throat gushing blood.

"Yvette!" she heard Julie scream.

Instantly, Yvette hopped up, staying close to the young teens. She saw Julie, gun in front of her, with Maurice behind her, and behind him was Michaels. He had both of his DE's pointed at the back of the child sex trafficker's lumped up and bleeding head.

"I'm good! We need an ambulance for these kids!" Yvette yelled.

Just then, she caught movement from above. The guard had the AR-15 pointed right at her. He smirked, seeing that he had her caught off guard.

Julie looked up and shrieked when she saw the guy.

BOOM!

The loud blast of a shotgun came. The guard's head exploded. His body fell over the loft's banister, landing with a bloody thud on the marble floor.

Michaels kicked Maurice in his back, making him fall face forward to the floor. He and Julie ran out from under the loft and pointed their guns up to the loft. Yvette's heart was beating so hard and fast. Her hands trembled. She could barely grip her gun.

A second later, as the three looked up at the loft, Lieutenant Sikes appeared, holding a tactical 12-guage shotgun.

"You all okay?" hollered down to them, looking at his handiwork.

"No," Yvette said through clenched teeth.

She marched off from where she was, heading straight for Maurice. Julie and Michaels stepped aside, out of her way. Maurice was attempting to get up when he saw Yvette coming. He couldn't move fast enough before she got to him.

CRACK!

She ran up on him, winding up like she was about to throw the first pitch at a softball game, and she smashed his jaw with her gun, completely shattering it.

Knocked clean out, Maurice dropped back down to the floor, asleep.

"How about now?" Sikes asked, coming down the stairs with his eyes on all the naked child molesters grouped in a corner, many of them with piss and feces at their feet.

"Nope," Yvette said. "Get the kids out of the room."

Julie and Lieutenant Michaels hurried to get the youngsters clothed and out of the penthouse. Yvette and Sikes looked at the thirteen creeps, with pure rage in their eyes.

BOC!

Yvette popped one in his dick. He screamed in pain as blood gushed down his legs.

BOOM!

Sikes opened the chest of the man closest to him, sending him flying backwards to the floor.

The eleven others tried to run out of fear. Yvette and Sikes squeezed their triggers over and over and over again. Sikes ran out of shells before Yvette, but the buck shots did what they were meant to do.

When the gun smoke cleared, they saw all the creeps looked like they had all been put in a blender and dumped out on the floor,

The penthouse's door opened up right then. Yvette and Sikes saw the two women that had the four of them on clean-up missions, enter the doorway in dark colored skirt suits and heels. With them were four men in suits, with earpieces in their ears.

The ladies pointed at Maurice.

"Take him to the chamber," Yvette heard Bernice order them.

She and Samantha then walked towards Yvette and Sikes. They both looked at them with sly smiles on their faces.

After a quick glance at the dead bodies, Samantha patted Yvette's arm.

"Good job," she said, stepping off with Bernice in tow. "No sense in standing around though. On with it."

When the ladies left with the men and Maurice, Yvette and Sikes exchanged glances.

"I don't like those old hoes," she told him.

He shook his head. "Me neither, but we need them, Jones."

She sighed to herself.

"For now… At least," Sikes added.

Yvette looked up at him and saw him smiling. She smiled right back at him.

"On to the next one," she then said, and made her way towards the doorway to head out, with Sikes right behind her.

Chapter 9

Phoenix grinned broadly at the sight before her. The giant warehouse she and her sisters, Venus and Star stood in was filled with expensive product just in off the boat from South America, that did not exist.

The cage closest to the three Salvadorian women had their most expensive import inside it, pacing back and forth, growling angrily.

"That is one angry kitty," Venus said with a sly smile.

"He's one big paycheck," Phoenix added, looking at the pissed off panther. "I'd hate to be whoever's buying him, though. He'll make dinner out of you, all of these precious pussy cats will."

Star's eyes gazed around the ten thousand-square-foot space, filled nearly to the brim with cages with exotic carnivorous felines, and other foreign animals, all of them smuggled into the country illegally.

Over ten million dollars' worth of animals were crammed into twenty cages. Jaguars, leopards, panthers, smaller cats, rare birds, different types of monkeys, and even a few marine mammals and fish.

Phoenix's team of exotic animal traffickers were assembled standing in a line like soldiers. Thirty brawny men, formerly members of military police units in El Salvador, were Phoenix's own personal mob of killers that did as she said, without hesitation, whether right, or wrong.

"Okay! Let's get ready! The transport will be here in five minutes!" Venus shouted to the men.

"Get 'em in and get them out!" Star then yelled.

"Muevanse!"

The men immediately obeyed. The sounds of their combat boots were the only sounds coming from them, as they began moving cages in line by order number, towards the row of loading dock doors.

"Jefa!"

Phoenix and her sisters heard one of the men yell just then. They turned and looked in the direction it had come from. They saw two of the other men, facing a female forward ahead of them, pointing their AK-47's at her back.

The three Salvadorenas looked at the woman. She was Asian, wearing a shirt that said, "Save the rain forest or we'll die!" with army fatigue pants and boots.

"Caught hey trying to free the gorilla!" the man told Phoenix.

They woman was pushed before the sisters. She scowled up at them.

"You wildlife freaks are really getting on my nerves," Phoenix said. She stepped down from the platform and walked up to the girl, dwarfing her by at least half a foot. "But it's okay, free food for these hungry cats."

Phoenix then saw the woman start smirking, as she looked up at her.

"I was thinkin' the same thing, bitch!" she said, her smirk turning into a diabolical smile.

Venus and Star saw the girl smile like a demented killer, right before their big sister reached into her suit jacket to pull her gun out.

In the blink of an eye, they saw the girl grab Phoenix's arm with enough force to make her spin around, then fold her arm behind her. The gun fell from Phoenix's hand. She screamed in pain as the girl twisted her arm.

"Shoot her! Matalaaa!" Phoenix cried to anyone.

Venus and Star upped their Taurus 9mm's and pointed but couldn't shoot. The risk of hitting their sister was too great. The men ran back to assist, all of them with assault rifles. The animals all went bananas, roaring, growling, howling, screeching.

"Sueltala ahora!" one of the men yelled, taking aim at the girl that had their boss hemmed up.

Suddenly, a pair of hands grabbed Venus from behind, at the same time as a pair grabbed Star. Both pairs snatched them up so quickly that they dropped their guns.

The men all turned to where their boss's younger sisters had been. They were no longer there.

Phoenix was in so much pain that her bladder let loose. She pissed down her pants suit leg, pooling inside of her high heels.

"I'm gonna teach you how it feels to be treated like a caged animal, bitch!" she heard the woman say in her ear, a second before one of her soldier's heads suddenly exploded, splattering all over the others' faces.

Julie snapped Phoenix's arm. She screamed at the top of her lungs when her bone cracked in half. Julie clipped her legs from under her, making her hit the floor as more silenced gunshots took out more of the armed men. The ones brave enough to stay while many others took off attempted to see where the shots were coming from.

PFFT! PFFT! PFFT!

Three more heads exploded. Five more men ran for their lives.

"Aaaaaaaaggghhhh!" Phoenix screamed, as Julie repeatedly stomped on the middle of her back.

CRACK!

With one final stomp, Julie crushed Phoenix's spine, paralyzing her from the waist down.

BRRRRRRRRRRR!

BRRRRRRRRRRRRRRRR!

Bullets from two choppers flew in Julie's direction. She dropped down, rolled towards where Phoenix's gun was, and landing on her stomach, caught one in her line of sight and fired, hitting him right in his nose.

His head snapped back as the slug blew through his head. His brains flew out the gaping hole, pieces of it landing in the cage with a jaguar. The cat immediately scarfed up the bloody chunks.

Julie rolled out of the way as two more of the soldiers started dumping at her. She came to a stop and hopped up, right as Lieutenant Michaels snuck up on one with a machete and sliced his head clean off, while Yvette drove an ice pick into the back of another's head, turning his lights off permanently.

The sounds of machine gunfire outside sounded like thunder booming. They heard screaming and crying for all of five seconds, before it and the shooting stopped.

Yvette snatched her pick out of the dead man's head, wiping the blood off on his shirt. She stood up and glanced around at all the animals.

"This is sad," she said to the lieutenant.

"Yep," he replied, then walked off towards where he and Yvette left Venus and Star immobilized by high voltage tasers and handcuffs.

***

Phoenix cried her eyes out. She couldn't move anything but her left arm, which she was using to hold her destroyed right arm.

Suddenly, she was yanked up from the floor as if she weighed nothing. The Asian girl appeared in front of her. She was not the one holding her up off the ground.

"Hi. So, you obviously know that you are fucked," the woman told her. "But I want you to see just how bad your senselessness is going to affect your little sisters."

103

The person holding her turned her, making her face the cage with the panthers, and one with a puma in it. She saw her sisters, both of them unconscious, being dragged towards the cages.

"N-n-noooo! Wait!" Phoenix cried.

The Asian girl walked off. She climbed up onto the cage with the puma in it. The big cat growled, swiping at the roof, its defensive instincts kicking in like a scared cornered dog.

Phoenix screamed and pleaded as Star was hoisted up onto the cage. The Asian girl unlatched the hatch in the roof and quickly pushed Star in with the meat-eater.

"Staaaarrr!"

Star began waking up. Her eyes opened a millisecond before the puma pounced on her. Phoenix watched in horror as the cat bit down on Star's face and started yanking and pulling. The blood-curdling screams that came from Star stopped seconds later, when her entire face was ripped off.

Venus woke up as she was being lifted up onto the panther's cage. She tried to fight for her life, but with her hands cuffed behind her back, all she had was her legs.

CRACK! CRACK! CRACK!

Julie socked Venus three quick times, dazing her enough to immobilize her. She then hurried and pushed her through the hatch, dropping her into the panther's space.

***

Yvette, Lieutenant Michaels, Julie and Lieutenant Sikes all watched the two vicious felines eat the two younger sisters' faces. It was like watching a ball python in a glass tank catch the food mouse, they were all geeked.

Phoenix cried her eyes out over her sisters. Lieutenant Sikes chuckled.

"Aww, don't cry. You'll be reunited with your dearly departed sisters in a minute," he told her, carrying her to the gigantic cage with the gorilla in it.

The monstrous ape snorted angrily. He growled, hitting his chest with massive fists. His sharp canine teeth were revealed when he roared with anger, remembering who was responsible for him being taken from his home, and who had constantly poked and prodded him with shock sticks.

"Say hello to Donkey Kong, bitch!" Julie hollered, opening the end of the cage.

"Noooooooooo!"

Sikes tossed her in and slammed the gate closed. They all watched the angry beast jump on her. He beat his chest, roaring out loudly, then as if it was made of a ball of butter, he brought his huge fist down on her face and completely obliterated her head.

The ape flattened nearly all of her, every time he brought a fist down. When he was done, he ripped a piece of flesh from her pancaked face and ate it. He looked at Yvette, Julie, Michaels, and Sikes. He snorted, then moved back to the corner, sitting down, and closing his eyes.

"Wow!" Yvette was beyond shocked to have just seen some shit like that in real life. "That was crazy!"

"Very!" Sikes agreed.

"I hope I never piss a gorilla off," Michaels said.

Julie started laughing. "I bet she ain't ever been pounded like that before."

All four of them busted out laughing their asses off at them, until they heard someone clearing their throat.

They turned their heads to the left. Samantha, Bernice and their men in black stood there, looking like government puppets.

"What's funny?" Samantha asked, with her hands on her hips.

"Yo' momma," Julie quipped, squeezing her nostrils closed with two fingers, to make her voice sound nasally.

Yvette and Sikes busted out laughing. Michaels snickered.

Samantha's and Bernice's eyebrows furrowed. Samantha stepped forward, approaching Julie.

"You keep talking shit and see where it gets you. I am the reason that you, your homegirl, your lieutenants, and your dope-dealer boyfriend and his homeboy aren't in jail, waiting to spend the rest of your lives in prison! What do you say to that, smart ass?"

Julie wrinkled her nose. "Your breath smells like cock. No wonder why you and Miss-Dick-Up-Her-Ass keep so many guys around you."

Yvette screamed out in laughter. Sikes wiped away the tears falling from his eyes from laughing so hard. Michaels laughed so hard that the gorilla started imitating him.

Even Bernice snickered, with their own squad trying not to, but failing miserably.

Samantha was steaming with anger.

"Make this the last crack you ever make, Tran, or you will go to prison," she said, turning on her snakeskin pumps. "Bitch!" she tossed over her shoulder, before walking off, switching her ass hard in the form-fitting wrap-dress she had on.

"Yo' momma!" Yvette hollered after her.

Bernice turned, trying to hide her smiling face. She beckoned to a few of her and Samantha's crew, while directing the others to get the animals to Customs.

"On to the next one, ladies," Michaels said.

"Uh-uh. Excuse me, Lieutenant, but I think we all need a break," Yvette said, missing her man so much. "We got time, seventy-two hours is what we need."

Michaels nodded. "Okay. We can take a break. We'll need a little time to prepare for the next one anyways. It's… um… tricky."

"Very," Sikes added.

"Bye, Donkey Kong!" Julie hollered to the gorilla, waving at him.

He waved back at her, imitating her hand movement.

The four left Samantha and Bernice's men to get the critters back where they belonged, and hopped into the stolen SUV's they'd pulled up in.

Yvette floored the Yukon's gas pedal, splitting off from their bosses to get on the highway and get out of Romeoville. Right away, they made calls to their dudes, dying to hear the sound of their voices.

***

"Haaaa! Aye, Joe, another attempt on Donald Cunt's life, fam!" T.G. shouted, laughing his ass off at the news feed on his Instagram.

Parked at a Pilot Travel Center truck stop, just outside of Indianapolis, T.G. and Bucks were both posted outside the Avalanche. Danny and ChaCha had their semis parked at the diesel pumps, fueling their tanks up. Javi had gone inside to grab everyone's orders of Chester's Chicken. Plans to push all the way to Atlanta before having to stop had been made. Neither Danny nor his wife wanted any trouble with state troopers. Random truck and trailer inspections would not be good.

"Get the fuck outta here!" Bucks said, shocked to hear that the two attempts of assassination had been made on the same presidential candidate, within months of each other.

"And!" T.G. added, showing his homie the screen to his iPhone. "It was another white guy! Tried to get him on a golf course!"

Bucks laughed his ass off. "Bitch ass was finna' get putted, dog! How many times does it take a man to come close to death for him to realize that he need to go sit his dumb ass down? Like for real, nigga… shit, fam! Does he not feel the fear that comes when a muhfucka realize that he can't go anywhere without someone tryna' blow him down?"

Just then, at the same exact time, T.G.'s and Bucks' phones rang. They both lit up with excitement when they saw it was their ladies. Answering, the two made their women unbelievably happy with empathic greetings. T.G. could hear the desire in Yvette's voice as she spoke about how much she missed him.

Bucks listened to Julie talk that freaky shit talk that she did so well. She had him ready to abandon the mission, hop a plane, and get back to her.

Javi approached just then, with three big bags of food.

"Let's ride, Joe," he told them, handing them their orders.

A truck air horn tooted a second later. They all turned to see ChaCha's Peterbilt rolling towards the exit, with Danny's Kenworth following.

"Bae, I'm bout to hit the road," T.G. said, hopping behind the wheel. "We stoppin' in Atlanta for the night. I'll call you from there."

"Okay, baby. Drive safe, buckle up and I love you," Yvette said.

T.G. chuckled. "Yes, ma'am, Miss Officer, and I love you too."

With Bucks in the back, Javi riding shotgun, T.G. pulled off to catch up with the rich, drug-trafficking trucker king and queen pin, anxious to get whatever mission done, so he could get back to his woman.

Chapter 10

Almost a day later, they arrived in Miami. Bucks and T.G. had never been to Florida before, let alone Miami. It looked just like what they saw on TV and in movies.

Behind the wheel, Javi followed ChaCha, now led by her husband down to an industrial section, close to the Port of Miami. Bucks, sitting in the back seat, saw tons of activity going on. He thought, wondering just how many trillions of dollars' worth of drugs and guns had gone through Miami, since whoever discovered it to be a port of entry for illegal goods to come in.

T.G. was thinking about how he might be able to possibly get Javi and his people to supply him and Bucks with the supreme A-1 cocaine that Flip told him the Valdez family were so famously known to have on deck, at all times.

***

Arriving at a big boat yard, tucked in the deep recesses of an area surrounded by swamps, with a single channel for boats to come in or sail out, Bucks and T.G. saw a few men in bright colored suits. One stood by a vintage 1960's era Shelby Cobra, joined by the two others, with a group of armed security.

They looked less than pleased when Javi and his cousins entered their yard.

"They look happy, huh?" Javi chuckled sarcastically, and he put the Avalanche in park behind ChaCha's rig.

"White people always look happy when niggas with money come around," T.G. said, glancing in his mirror at the tinted vehicle, hiding in plain sight.

"They are all from Spain," Javi corrected, watching the man he knew to be the leader, stay by his Bugatti Chiron, while two of his men went to Danny's truck and ChaCha's. "And they are all in violation. Keep y'all eyes open, follow yo' instincts, and don't die."

Bucks reached down and grabbed the Taurus .40 caliber, and the Taurus' "Judge" that had come out of the custom gun rack under the rear seat, cocking the .40 back and tucking it in his waistline. By his left foot, standing up, was the biggest machine gun he had ever had the pleasure of possessing in his life.

T.G., armed with the same weapons, was ready to get on some gangster shit. He wanted to earn the connect so badly that he was willing to pop everyone that was not a friend of Javi's, or his people.

***

"Lleva tu camion al interior de la casa de botes," Hector said to the big man behind the wheel of the first semi-truck.

The guy nodded his head. He shifted into first gear and rolled off, towards the gargantuan indoor boat storage warehouse, where the land entrance door was being opened by a couple of the big boss's goons.

Looking to his right, where Guillermo had given the same directive to the driver of the second rig, Hector stood where he was and caught a glimpse of the driver. His eyes went wide with shock when he saw the blue-eyed beauty behind the wheel.

Dios Mio! Que mujer mas hermosa! he thought, gobsmacked by her.

Guillermo approached, looking at the black Chevy Avalanche that had pulled in with the big rigs. But behind the Avalanche, he swore he peeped an older SUV following too.

"These people drive really fancy trucks," he said to Hector, who was looking towards where their boss stood at his car. "Es inteligente hacerlo con un monton de cocaina en sus remolques?"

Hector shrugged as the sound of Francisco's Cobra's engine firing up. Guillermo looked again for the old SUV but no longer saw it.

"Those Latin Negroes have been transporting cocaine in those fancy trucks for decades. The police are afraid of them, but we are not."

The Cobra rolled past them, vibrating the ground under their feet. Guillermo grew nervous as he and Hector watched their boss head towards the boat house.

"Crees que ellos saben que fuimos hostros los que hicimos estallar su club, con toda esa gente dentro?" he asked Hector.

"Who cares. If they do know, they'll assume Francisco was the one that ordered it, then they kill him, and we take over everything."

Hector and Guillermo went and hopped into their cars. In his gleaming new Ferrari Roma, Hector cruised to the boat house with Guillermo behind him in his 1988 Lamborghini Countach. They pulled into the boat house and parked next to Francisco. The garage was closed, with only the three bosses inside and a few of their goons, along with the two Valdez truckers.

***

Francisco looked at the beautiful woman that got out of the second rig. He was stunned. The jean bodysuit she had on clung to her shapely physique like it was a second skin.

Her hair up in a high ponytail made her look like an innocent schoolgirl, but he could tell she was far from it, from how tall she was in her thuggish Timberland boots.

The sound of the door from the rig up front closing averted to the humongous man climbing down from the cab. Francisco curled his lip up, sneering at the guy with pure malice in his eyes.

Hector and Guillermo, joined by four of their armed comrades, joined him at his side as the husband-and-wife duo made their way to him.

"Thank you for coming. I wasn't expecting the boss and his wife to be who shows up with my shipment," Francisco said to Daniel and Ximena Valdez, with a shit-eating grin on his face.

"Expect the unexpected, my man," Danny told him with a smirk.

CRACK!

Out of nowhere, ChaCha cocked back and rocked Francisco's jaw. Hector and Guillermo gasped from the rudeness of the punch. Their men, caught off guard by it, faltered as they attempted to defend their bosses.

ChaCha dove forward and from her hands, catapulted herself up high in the air. Hector and Guillermo and their goons looked up at her, so distracted that none of them saw Danny.

Guillermo's throat was instantly crushed when Danny punched him in his Adam's apple. He grabbed at it, struggling to breathe through his destroyed windpipe. ChaCha landed on one of the shooter's shoulders, and faster than he could have anticipated, she let herself drop after she locked her legs around his neck, killing him instantly.

The other shooters all jumped back and took aim at her and Danny, while Hector ran to grab the boss and get him up out of there.

BRRRRRRRRRRRRRR!
BRRRRRRRRRRRRRR!

BRRRRRRRRRRRRR!
BRRRRRRRRRRRRRR!
BRRRRRRRRRRRRRRR!
Bucks, T.G. and Javi squeezed and swept left and right. The huge fully automatic machine guns M249's spit round after round from the 200-round boxes they were equipped with.

Alongside Bucks and T.G., were two men with long dreads, golden-brown skin, built like body builders. The five of them sent slugs flying at all the Argentinean goons that seemed to keep coming from every nook and cranny the boat house had.

***

Hector howled in pain as a bullet slammed into his right ass cheek. He dropped Francisco back to the ground, falling down next to him. He clutched his bleeding ass, rolling around on the ground in agony.

A pair of Timberlands appeared by his face. Hector looked up into the piercing artic blue eyes of the female trucker, who stood next to her husband.

"Maybe next time you'll think about blowing up a club that I own, mal parido!" she snapped, cursing like a Colombian.

"It was Francisco's idea!" Hector lied. "I swear!"

"Well," Danny chimed in. "It is now my idea to choose the way you die. Hmmmm… oohh, wait! I got it!"

The ridiculously strong six-foot-four giant grabbed Hector up off the ground like he was as light as a teddy bear. He was dragged to the trailer that was hooked up to the Kenworth the Valdez family's head honcho drove.

Hector saw the five other guys dragging the still unconscious Francisco, along with the asphyxiated Guillermo, and the few shooters who had not caught bullets.

The Dominican cocaine kingpin's wife clutched one of the M249's, eyes open, shifting around, ready to dead anyone dumb enough to show their face.

"Wait! What are you doing?" Hector asked, regretting the day he had gone to work for Francisco, as the man opened the trailer's doors.

Being dragged to the rear of the trailer, leaving a booty-blood trail behind, Hector attempted to get up and get out of there.

"Come on, man," the giant said, grabbing him, and tossing him up inside the long cargo space. "Dumbass Spanish cracker," he called him then.

Francisco, finally regaining consciousness, opened his eyes as he was thrown inside. Guillermo's lifeless body landed on top of him. Their only remaining shooters were forced inside by gun point.

"I will kill you all!" Francisco declared, with a splitting headache.

"Shut up, bitch!" Bucks shot back and popped him in his kneecap.

Francisco dropped to the trailer floor, screaming with pain, bleeding profusely.

"Where are you taking us?" Hector demanded to know.

"To another time zone, mamahueo," Danny told him with a sneaky smirk, then he closed the trailer doors.

It was pitch-black inside. Francisco, Hector and their goons heard nothing but each other breathing. Then came clanging and banging. Minutes after, diesel engines started and began revving up loudly.

"Oh, sshhit!" Hector panicked when he and the others felt the trailer drop and hit the ground.

The truck engines faded away in seconds. It went dead silent for nearly a minute, then the sounds of beeping came from the gig wooden crate inside the trailer with them.

It took Francisco, Hector and their guys a matter of seconds to realize what was inside the crate.

"Dios Mio!" Francisco panicked, pissing in his pants.

Hector closed his eyes and started praying. He might as well, because he knew it was over with.

***

T.G. floored it behind the old 80's Chevy Suburban, with ChaCha behind him, and Danny bringing up the rear, neither of them coupled to the trailers they had pulled from Illinois.

T.G. followed the old steel rammer out of the boat yard and onto the road that ran next to it.

"Three!" Javi counted, hanging out of the passenger's window, waiting to see the grand finale. "Two! On—"

BOOM!

The bombs inside both of the trailers exploded with such a powerful blast that it leveled the building and created a deep crater in the ground.

Debris flew everywhere like a tornado, tossing everything it sucked up into its funnel. A severed arm, severely burned, landed on the windshield.

"Damn. What the hell was in those crates, fam?" Bucks asked Javi.

"A whooole 'lotta don't ever try us again, bitch," Javi told him. "And for the record… you and yo' guy have successfully passed our test. We are at your disposal, my niggas."

"Period," T.G. said with a smile. "But you, Javi. There's somethin' else I wanted to ask you, bruh."

"Yes."

"Huh?" T.G. glanced over at him, then back out the rear of the rammer.

"You want a plug on that pollito. Yes. I got you. Now stay on my cousin's bumper. We finna' slide on over to Star Island while the cops clean up that red rain falling from the sky," Javi said, pulling out his iPhone to call his wife.

T.G. and Bucks were geeked. They now had the best connect on the best cocaine, that either made people ridiculously rich, or got them killed from greed and treachery. They couldn't wait to flood the streets with the superb Valdez product and take in the dough by the truckload.

***

They made it to a colossal trucking yard just down the road from the port. T.G. saw "PJ & D Transport, LLC" on a sign posted outside of the business's perimeter fence. Hundreds of semis and trailers were inside, many coming or going. It was like a small trucker city.

"This is yo' cousin's business, Javi?" Bucks asked, as T.G. floored the Suburban, while he peeped Danny and ChaCha break off and head towards a big diesel repair garage.

"Yep. Started by my grandpa and his brothers, back before we was even born. Them muhfuckas did they thang, Bucks, put us all up for life and provided us with opportunities to provide opportunities for others that will actually do somethin' with themselves, 'ya dig?'"

T.G. and Bucks both understood. They had always heard how gracious the big Dominican family was. They were the richest and most selfless family to arise from Santo Domingo. They were also the most ruthless if they were put on anyone's asses. Nobody survived.

***

The two light-skinned dreadheads hopped out of the steel rammer, just outside of what looked like a jet hanger. T.G. looked at them, both now just in tank tops. Their massive arms were tatted, looking like inked-up pythons and anacondas. With massive, tatted chests, their physiques looked like they were professional gym rats.

"Bro, who is they, though?" T.G. asked Javi as he parked on the right side of the 'Burban. "Them niggas look wild as fuck."

"They are two out of seven members of the Steel City Mafia," Javi told him, opening his door. "And my big cousins. You are most definitely correct, too. Them the wildest muthafuckas you will ever meet, fam."

T.G. and Bucks got out of the Avalanche. Javi introduced his older cousins to them. The two SCM goons' presence was intimidating, without even saying a word. When they dapped and embraced Bucks and T.G., it was like a huge weight lifted off their chests, to know that the two dreadlocked monsters were allies.

Macho, standing six-three, and his slightly older six-foot-six brother Tool, were half Dominican, half Puerto Rican, born and raised in Pittsburgh, Pennsylvania. Not many other hood niggas compared to them. They were both billionaire cocaine gods, but unlike those who had obtained that status, the bluish-gray-eyed Macho, and his Waka Flocka Flame-clone brother were still in the trenches, and neither of them gave a fuck about who felt like they should fall back and let goons handle their opps. They were raised as goons and would die as goons. Period.

"Good to meet y'all, yo'," said Macho. "It's always good to meet a couple of guys we been hearin' about, shaking' shit up and makin' wannabes bow to y'all. Hats off to you two."

Bucks and T.G. were bewildered to hear those words come from the maniacal demon like Macho Valdez. There were a lot of stories about him, his wife and his girlfriend. Props from him, was like an up-and-coming rapper without a deal, being approached by Jigga himself, seeking a session with him.

"We just gettin' how we live, fam," T.G. said modestly. "Like anybody that's stuck in the mud should do."

"Humble too," Tool spoke, in a deep raspy voice, nodding his head at them.

"Well, it should be obvious that this task could've been done in-house, 'yah mean?'" Macho said. "But when my cousins hit me 'n my bro up, and said y'all so bravely rode up in a Lyft on Michelle's property, which is standing on top of a lot of bones, I was like, bet! Bring 'em in, let's see if they can hang wit' some real goons on a whole new level. And y'all did. So now, y'all are gon' be good. We got ya' backs, and we got y'all ladies backs too."

Bucks and T.G. both nodded their heads in appreciation. Being recruited into the Valdez family circle was the same as MJ being inducted into the Hall of Fame.

"Oye, tiguerasos!" Javi hollered out. "Congratulations. Y'all in the big leagues now. Let's go see what that looks like."

Macho and Tool led them into the garage, and out to the back. A big boat dock was there, leading out to the open waters. Moored at the dock was a 2020, hundred and five-foot Numarine yacht. More than eleven million dollars' worth of luxury floated, waiting to take them to the residential island where only the riches of the rich lived.

Chapter 11

Macho manned the helm of his yacht and sailed over to Star Island. Docking at the rear of his enormous $200 million dollar mansion, spanning 22,750 square feet, he and his brother moored the yacht to the dock, then they and Bucks and T.G., Danny and ChaCha disembarked.

Taking it all in, Bucks and T.G. were awestruck by the palatial dwelling. It looked like something Oprah would live in. Even the green grass looked luxurious.

The rear of the house had the most remarkable back yard. Beyond the wide-open grassy field, a lagoon with a custom waterslide, surrounded by lounging chairs and picnic tables.

An infinity edge pool was built on the all-marble patio deck, just outside the steps that led up to the custom stone lanai. Tall glass doors to the spacious interior began retracting as they all walked through the glass towards the house.

"What the fuck?" Bucks said to himself, when he saw amongst two big Rottweilers, a red nosed Pit Bull, three Cane Corsos, a Presa Canario and a snow leopard, run out of the mansion, down the steps, right towards them.

T.G.'s instincts were to run but wasn't outrunning any of the animals. He then recognized two of the Cane Corsos from the diamond jewelry store that belonged to Javi's wife.

Right behind the animals, Bucks and T.G. saw Javi's wife, holding the hands of a little boy that looked just like him, and a little dark-brown-skinned girl, that didn't look like Javi nor Michelle. Along with Michelle, they saw eight more women, each of them so damn gorgeous that it was like watching an episode of *Cartel Crew*, Afro-Latina edition. The women all had one or two young children with them, with the exception of the last woman, whose stomach was as big as a beach ball.

"Hold up… aye? Is that ol' girl from *Wild 'N Out*?" T.G. asked Javi, looking at the redhead that held the hand of a little girl, while a teenage girl walked next to her. "And Lauren London?" he added, looking at another chick.

Javi, Macho, Tool, Danny and ChaCha busted out laughing as the fur posse finally reached them and excitedly yipped, snorted and grunted.

"Everyone thinks Kenzie is Justina Valentine's clone," ChaCha informed T.G., "until they see all that shape she has. Kenzie is Xavier's wife. The other chick is Nena, she is one of Xavier's baby mamas, and so is my cousin, Vanessa."

Macho excitedly showered his hyper chocolate tiger-striped female Pit Bull, named Dreams with love and affection, along with the snow leopard he had bought for his wife, named Sky, and his wife's purebred German Rottweiler, Maliante.

Javi's dogs Dream and Diamond jumped around him as he play-boxed with them. ChaCha's massive tiger striped Presa Canario, named Pablo, barked as deeply as a Great Dane, happy as hell his humans were back. Tool's Rottweiler, Angel, who was Maliante's daughter, enjoyed a belly rub from her owner, laying on her side in the grass.

The other Cane Corso stuck to the side of her human, a maple-syrup complexioned Latina with the shape of an hourglass, accentuated by the brilliant white shoulder-less bodysuit she had on, with white, Red Bottom sneakers, and her brown-dyed hair in long boxed braids, balled and styled up on the top of her head.

***

Meeting the eight beautiful ladies by the lagoon, Bucks and T.G. were introduced to them all. Macho introduced his gorgeous caramel Nuyorican wife Yessina, along with her and his six-year-old twin daughters Jazmine and Yazmine. With Yessy and their little ladies was Gabriella, aka G-Baby. She was a Chicagorilla, Puerto Rican like Yessy. Her Cane Corso, named Fendi, because of the colors of her tiger-striped fur matching the highly coveted designer's main colors, stuck to her side like she was glued to the voluptuous Boricua.

Bucks and T.G. were floored to learn that Yessy was Macho's wife and G-Baby was his girlfriend, all of them in a three-way relationship that had come a long way, with a lot of drama to follow.

G-Baby had her own six-year-old twins with Macho. Nova and Nona looked like their mother but had their father's wild side embedded in them.

Bucks and T.G. were then introduced to Javi's youngest sister Evelyn, and her long-time lover, Gloria, both Dominicanas. Evelyn, light brown like her brother with a retro hairstyle, dyed poison green and shaved on the right side, was a wild Cardi B type chick. Her girlfriend, Gloria, a milk chocolate toned chick that wore her hair in a spiral curled afro to embrace her African roots, was quiet, but so very deadly, especially when it came to any other woman or man, that tried to get at her woman. Evelyn and Gloria were joined by the four-year-old they had recently adopted, named Cecilia.

Tool's dark chocolate and very pregnant Belizean wife, Tamalita, was introduced to Bucks and T.G., then the three women, two of them the baby mamas of Xavier, Vanessa and Nena and Xavier's wife, Kenzie.

Vanessa's daughter with Xavier, Gianna, had both her Puerto Rican and Persian mother's features, and her Dominican father's as well.

The Black, Mexican and Greek Nena, a dead ringer for the *ATL* star actress, and her son Jordan, had similar physical features, but he had the strong and silent personality of his father.

The Cuban-Armenian redhead, whom Xavier had fallen so hard in love with, was now his loving wife. They had been the most unlikely to marry, if you had asked his family. Between Kenzie, and her now fourteen-year-old daughter Neveah, who Xavier had rescued from Kenzie's abusive and deranged baby daddy, when Neveah was just five years of age. ChaCha's younger cousin, Vanessa and the New New replica, the Valdez clan all thought the former Valdez playboy would've wed Vanessa, his childhood sweetheart. They all realized how much Xavier loved Kenzie, even with a bodily malfunction that would make most men run for the hills. When she disappeared, ghosting him for two years, then out of nowhere, popped up with a two-year-old claiming that she was Xavier's daughter, Faith, he took Kenzie back, and cherished her and his daughters, like a real man does, when he truly loves a woman.

***

After Bucks and T.G. met the notorious main circle of the family, all the crazy stories they heard about the wild and wealthy Afro-Latinos, they believed, but also, they saw just how real a family they all were. The love and compassion that Bucks and T.G. saw, made them wish for the day that they were blessed with their own children, brought into the world by the two amazing women they loved with all of their hearts.

***

"Oye, 'mano?" Javi walked up to Buck and T.G. "What's good with y'all? Y'all niggas look like a muhfucka rained on yo' parade," he said with his wife, their son Javi Jr., and Javi's daughter Amara, who had come into the world by his adulterous ways.

Demon and Diamond stood by their kids' sides, enjoying getting behind their ears scratched.

Bucks shrugged. "I just wish my girl was here, Javi," he admitted.

"Straight up," said T.G., missing his crazy firecracker.

"Check it out, yo," said Macho, waking up, holding his twins Jazmine and Yazmine in his big ass arms. "How about y'all go on ahead in the crib and get some rest? Y'all had quite a rough month. Go decompress, take showers, I got some swag up there in each closet that will fit y'all. We'll all be here when you two handle 'ya bizness, then later on, we can all sit and rap about what the future holds."

Bucks and T.G. both nodded their heads and thanked the two color-eyed cousins. Macho gave them directions to where their rooms were, then they both headed off, ready to recharge their batteries, drained of all energy from non-stop drama.

***

Astounded was the only word to describe how Bucks and his brother from another mother felt as they made their way through the grand mansion. They both surmised that A-list celebrities would pine for Macho's spot.

Taking the glass elevator up to the second floor from the expansive open-concept main level, they made their way towards the long hallway, with ten big guest bedrooms. Bucks dapped his guy up, then they headed to the rooms Macho had set up for them.

***

"Holy Shit!" Bucks blinked his eyes, unwilling to believe what he was seeing. After five times, nothing had changed. "Whaaaat!" he shouted, his shocked expression turning into a ginormous smile.

"Hey, handsome," purred Julie, posing on the bed, wearing a sexy red lace bra and thong set, with a garter belt clipped to red thigh-high fishnet stockings, and red patent leather pumps.

Rock was laid out on the bed with the red-hot vixen, tail wagging excitedly when he saw Bucks.

"How the… Naw… I'm dreamin'. You are not really here," he said, thinking he had to be way past exhausted.

But then Julie got up off the bed and went to him. She pulled him down by the collar of his shirt and kissed him. She took his hands and placed them on her perky little apple bottom while they tongued each other down.

A minute later, Julie pulled back. She looked up at him with a seductive smile.

"Still think I'm not here, baby?" she asked, wrapping her arms around his neck.

"Hmmm… I think… if I slid up in that wet ass pussy this figment of my imagination that looks like my woman might have, then I might believe that she's really here."

Julie giggled. She reached her hands down and undid his jeans, dropping them and his boxers to his ankles. Bucks felt her hand wrap around his hardness. She sank down to her knees and planted a kiss on the tip of it.

Looking up at him, Julie asked, "Are we getting there yet?" She opened her mouth, stuck her tongue out, and engulfed all ten of his inches.

Bucks shuddered. "Shit! I… wooo! I… mmm… we… almost! Fuck!" he cursed, as she deep throated him, slowly, making love to his cock with her mouth.

Julie planned to do way more to her man, after being deprived of his love for too many days, and in the room adjacent to where they were, she knew her best friend and secret lover was doing the same with her man.

***

T.G.'s eyes rolled to the back of his head as Yvette's warm, skilled mouth pleasured him. Her glossy red lips, wrapped around his throbbing cock, was as visually as pleasing to see as the feeling itself.

When he walked into the bedroom, he was shocked when Sir ran up to him. Thinking he really needed some sleep, he brushed Sir off as just a mirage, until Yvette emerged from the bathroom, wearing nothing but red patent leather thigh-high stripper boots, and red lipstick with her hair looking wet wild and tantalizingly sexy. He went to rush her, but she beat him to it and pounced on him like a hungry lioness on a foolish antelope out in the open Sahara plains by itself.

In a matter of seconds, T.G. was stripped of his shoes and clothes and leaning against the main wall by the built-in eighty-five-inch HDTV. Yvette, on her knees before him, had no problem taking his thick ten-inch pipe to the back of her throat. With one hand, she cupped and massaged his balls. T.G. groaned, his toes curling as she domed him up.

Minutes later, he couldn't take it anymore. He pulled his dick out of her mouth, scooped her up from her knees and took her to the bed. He climbed on top and kissed her lips, down to her neck, to her breasts. He sucked each of her nipples, rubbing one while orally pleasing the other. Yvette arched off the bed, moaning in bliss. She called his name repeatedly, begging him to go lower.

T.G. took his time, though. He wanted her to be blazing hot. Slowly, he kissed his way down her flat stomach. She shrieked and giggled when he stuck his tongue in her belly button, then motorboated it.

He continued traveling south. Pushing her legs wide open, he exposed her dripping wet love box. He licked up her juices, relishing the taste of her nectar. Yvette trembled, feeling him plant soft kisses on her inner thighs. Her clit swelled, throbbing, aching for his lips and tongue. But he resisted her urges, and continued kissing her thighs, licking each one. Only when Yvette nearly cried from how bad she wanted his face in it, did T.G. finally give her what she wanted.

T.G. pushed her legs out as wide as they would go, then lowered his face down to her soaking wet pussy, ready to eat her up like she was filet mignon.

***

"Mmmmmm, Bernaaard! Oooooo! Shit!" cried Julie, face down, ass up, with Bucks' tongue swirling around her puckered asshole.

She buried her face in the bed sheet as he ate her ass like he loved doing. She had never been able to stop being so amazed at how freaky Bucks was. Whether he was sucking on her clit, eating her ass, or piping her down, he did it all well, and made her feel like her legs didn't work after she orgasmed.

Bucks licked and slurped all through her ass crack, then he rose up, gripping his hardness, ready to slide up in her wet-wet from the back.

Julie bit her bottom lip, feeling him enter her. He filled her up, hitting the bottom of the pussy. He started stroking it, slowly, holding onto her hips as he loved her.

Julie cried out his name repeatedly, screaming how much she loved him. He hollered it back, gritting his teeth, feeling her pussy muscles clenching around his cock. She was so wet that he made her pussy fart as he pounded it. Minutes later, she climaxed so hard that for seconds after, she went blind.

Bucks kept on pounding her after she came. Feeling his own nut rising, he flipped her, put her on her back and climbed on top. He slid right back in, grabbed her leg and folded her knee up, then he jackhammered the pussy. Just as he exploded, cumming deep inside of her, Julie reached another orgasm, exploding like the blowhole of a blue whale, all over his dick.

They both plopped down next to each other, breathing hard, sweaty, hearts racing, their eyes looked deep into each other's. A moment of silence passed between them, while they peered into each other's eyes, soul searching with each other.

Then Julie broke the silence.

"I'm pregnant, Bernard," she revealed.

Bucks' eyes went as wide as dinner plates. "Wh-what?"

She smiled at him. "We're gonna have a baby, baby."

Overwhelmed with joy, Bucks pulled her to him and hugged her up in his arms. Julie's eyes welled with tears of happiness. When she learned of the reason that she kept getting sick, Yvette suggested a pregnancy test.

When they both saw the word "PREGNANT" pop up, they were both shocked beyond belief. Neither of them had ever pictured themselves as mothers. Just two bad bitches with guns having fun and getting money.

But that changed, the moment they saw the results of the endless fucking and lovemaking. Julie cried, beyond thankful that the father was the love of her life. She couldn't wait to tell him, but she didn't want to reveal it over the phone, nor did she want to wait.

Yvette contacted a mutual friend, whom she knew was in tune with who T.G. and Bucks were with. The mutual friend got her in contact with Macho Valdez, and it was immediately set up for her and Julie to fly down and give their men the biggest surprise ever.

"I can't believe this! I'ma be a daddy? For real, though?" Bucks asked, holding his woman close to his heart.

"Yes, baby! You are! A great daddy!" Julie cried, feeling like she was on top of the world.

Bucks kissed her and thanked her repeatedly. He never pictured himself having a child. Having one with the most gorgeous gangster chick in the world, it couldn't get any better than that.

***

Yvette screamed out at the top of her lungs, head held back, face up, as she climaxed all over T.G.'s cock while she bounced up and down on him. T.G. exploded inside of her, planting his seed deep inside.

Winded, Yvette laid down on top of him and kissed his lips as the sound of Ginuwine's "ROLE PLAY" crooned from the built-in home audio system. She couldn't get enough of his touch. She couldn't get enough of him. She couldn't wait to see a positive pregnancy test of her own, and she couldn't wait for the day a big diamond ring got put on her finger.

"What did you do to me, Tremaine?" asked Yvette, gazing down into his eyes.

"You mean before, or after I got the pussy for the first time?" he asked her with a chuckle.

Yvette laughed at him. "You're funny, dude. It ain't just the sex that has me feelin' the way I do though, bae. You really mean everything to me."

T.G. started smiling. He wrapped his arms around her, holding her naked body to his own.

"You're my air, Yvette. I can't breathe without you, baby. Real nigga shit."

For a second, she twisted her lips up at him, then she gave her reply.

"So, why you leave me hangin' in Jamaica, after JuJu and I saved you and Bucks from yo' guy's crooked-ass daddy?" she wanted to know.

"Because you made me mad. Duh, muhfucka."

Yvette mushed his face. "Shut up."

"You asked me a question and got an answer."

"You know what I mean, Tremaine. Don't be a booty-hole, nigga, or I'll bite cho' muthafuckin' nose and rip it off."

"Then how I'ma smell you when you wear sexy perfume? And how I'ma smell my pussy before I eat it up?"

Yvette busted out laughing. "God, I love yo' crazy ass, baby," she told him.

He pulled her down and got another kiss, then smacked her ass, palming and squeezing her meaty cheeks.

"How long is it gon' take for you, JuJu, and y'all's bosses to be back good?" he asked them.

"We got a few more people to get at for these two weird-ass bitches. Our boss swears up and down that they got power like the CIA."

"Must be true, 'cause none of us are locked up. The news stopped broadcastin' our photos and now it's some other people they lookin' for, that's probably already dead."

"The feds got their hands full. Mr. King of New York, people steady tryna' take Donald Punk's head off, the opioid epidemic, we gon' be alright. Trust me, baby."

"We most definitely gon' be alright, love. Bucks and I got the connect with Javi and Macho."

Yvette went wide eyed. "Whoa… that is big. They make Benicio and his people look like a corner-store gang when you compare them to the Cartel Jalisco Nuevo Generaccion."

T.G. laughed his ass off. "That's cold, bae."

She shrugged. "I don't give a fuck."

"Well. Hopefully, this bullshit can get handled sooner than later, me and bro ready to flood the whole Lake County with that supreme shit them niggas got so much of."

And I'm ready to have your baby, Yvette thought, gazing down into his eyes again, so in love with the man that she just could not picture life without him.

Chapter 12

One Week Later…

"Maaaan, oh maan, oh maaan! Joe! Look at this shit, fam! That shit look like my version of white-gold!" Flip exclaimed, as he saw two hundred bricks of Dominican cocaine, sitting on a wooden pallet, fresh off the big rig as it came into the auto detailing garage that T.G. and Bucks both invested in.

Standing inside, T.G., Bucks, Flip, Low, and GB were stuck in awe, looking at all the cocaine. Each of them had already started doing numbers in their heads.

Twenty-thousand a brick! *Fuck it*! *This the cream of the crop right here, Joe*! T.G. thought.

Niggas is gon' be mad as fuck when we take over. And we got the realest goon squad on earth holdin' us down…yeah… it's on, thought Bucks.

Flip, Low, and GB were ready to put word out that they had that click-clack-pow-knock-a-bitch-down. They had clucks in every neighborhood and town all over northern Illinois, that nearly flew to them when they let it be known that they had Paris Hilton and Lindsey Lohan combined on deck, but what they had always heard about the Valdez coke, they knew that they now had that Pamela Anderson on deck.

"Aye, Joe. Fuck this standin' around shit," Flip said, rubbing his hands together. "Let's buss' these muhfuckas down and hit 'em up! I'm ready to get this money!"

"Let's do it," Bucks replied. "Ready as well."

***

With the shop down for the night, a group of young hungry wolves posted outside in the shadows, strapped like they were old war veterans with PTSD and schizophrenia. T.G., Bucks, and their homies got to it. They broke down bricks of raw, cut them up with special ingredients for the snorters, and for the smokers, straight coke, no cut, and baking soda.

By the time daybreak came, they had almost two bricks cooked up into crack, and five kilos of raw turned into ten, with the potency still high enough to turn clear plastic yellow.

They all looked at what they had cooked up, then what they had left.

"Cocaine won't spoil… will it?" Low asked.

They all looked at him, as if he had just asked the dumbest question ever.

Flip, GB, and Low started putting the word out for their clucks to "Come 'N Get It!" Within minutes, their phones were blowing up. T.G. and Bucks watched them put orders together, then one by one, armed with two pistols, extra clips, and hunting knives, they headed out to hit the streets.

T.G. and Bucks sent word to some of their own people. Right away, requests for ounces and bigger orders came in. They each got enough for three clients each, not wanting to ride too dirty, then strapping up, they hopped into their whips and headed off to go check into cash.

***

"Noooo!"

BOCKA!

The young woman's scream was silenced when the big Greek goon put a hot one in her brain, rocking her to sleep forever.

Her head snapped back, skull fragments and brains splattered on the clean white plastic stretched out behind her, put there purposely to contain her remnants.

"Okay, Doc. She's all yours," George said, stepping back with his Berretta still smoking.

Doctor Allen and his team of nurses hurried to grab the dead Filipino girl. They hoisted her up and laid her on the operating table. Doctor Allen then hurried to wash and sterilize his hands, then his head nurse assisted him by putting on his gloves.

"Alrighty, people!" he said as another nurse rolled over a tray with operating tools laid out on it. "Let's clean this girl out, we've got a very rich customer in need of her parts, way more than she does."

George went outside of the makeshift operating room to smoke a cigarette. Already there were his four friends that had created the highly profitable ring of trafficking human organs on the black market along his side. Ezekiel, Titus, Bartholomew, and Stefano were smoking cigarettes and conversating amongst each other, when the top dog emerged.

"Such a shame," George said, flaming up a cowboy-killer. "That little bitch was a beautiful girl. I should've sampled her before I killed her."

Ezekiel looked at him. "She was just fifteen years old, George."

George blew out a lungful of smoke. "Does it look like I care? Pussy is pussy, young, old, brown, black, purple… as long as my cock gets wet, I will put it in anything that makes me cum," he said, casting a side glance at the long-haired Stefano, with a sly smirk on his face.

Stefano tried to hide the smile that threatened to come out. Ezekiel and Titus both shuddered, knowing that George and Stefano got down with each other. It sickened them, but the amount of money they made by snatching up lost souls and selling their organs to wealthy folks that weren't ready to die from organs failing them and unwilling to wait for years for a kidney or a liver, ruled how the two dealt with the two homosexuals, ignoring what did not pertain to them.

***

The buzzing of the garage door sounded off just then. George went to the video screens by the security camera system. He saw the black van that brought new money in, ready to back in and unload.

"Another shipment is here," he announced, hitting the button to open the garage up. "It must be the Somalians."

His associates tossed their squares to the ground and stepped on them as the van backed inside. George closed the garage door when it was backed up to the ledge of the elevated dock he and his men stood on.

George went to greet the driver. When the tall slender white man with freckles, and an orangish-red beard got out, wearing mechanic coveralls, he frowned. His matching hair was slicked back with gel, parted up one side.

"Where is Gregory?" George asked, not liking the fact that the normal transporter was not there.

"He is sick, I am Arnold Pish, his replacement," the man told him. "Normally, I am… he who hunts to retrieve what is on your grocery list."

George nodded his head. He knew what the guy was saying, the man was his body snatcher.

"Okay. Let's get ya unloaded and back on your way. Ezekiel, Titus, Bart, why don't you lend Mr. Pish a hand, while Stefano and I go see how the doctor is doing?"

Titus curled his lip up, shuddering at the thought. He and the other two stepped up while George headed towards a set of doors, with Stefano hot on his trail.

The driver grabbed the handle to the van's rear doors, then yanked the right one open, startling the three Greeks.

Then suddenly, a big German Shepherd flew out of the van like a cannonball fired out of a cannon. Before Ezekiel could even process the danger, the dog jumped on his and took him to the ground, sinking his teeth into his right arm and trying to rip it clean out of his socket.

The other two were so shocked that they hadn't even seen the other German Shepherd, nor the Belgian Malinois jump out of the van, three more people emerged. Ezekiel, Titus, and Bartholomew caught a glimpse of the two women, the taller older Black man that came out of the van, while the driver removed his fake beard and the slick-back wig.

***

Yvette and Julie watched as Sir, Rock and Ranger made the organ traffickers curry. Lieutenant Sikes smiled, watching his significantly smaller dog do as much damage as the two bigger GSDs. Lieutenant Michaels wished his dog was a killer, but bis wife had only trained Damar to be a couch potato that looked vicious.

The ladies called their dogs off after the two men they were mauling pissed and shitted in their pants. Lieutenant Sikes let Ranger continue ripping the man's throat until he had torn it completely out.

"I'll go find the other two," Sikes said, calling his dog to his side. "Deal with the medical staff."

With his dog, Sikes grabbed his tactical Mossberg pump from the van, then hurried off through the doors he had seen the other two Greeks run through.

Yvette, Sir, Julie, Rock, and Michaels headed off, creeping quietly into the main hallway, with AR-15s, fitted with suppressors and red beams.

Remembering the blueprints of the abandoned building that Samantha and Bernice had gotten for them, Yvette led the way. She stayed low as she moved, gun up, finger around the trigger.

Julie and Michaels followed, Sir and Rock, instinctively in "work" mode walked so that their nails didn't tap on the shined-up floor.

A woman exited the room, wearing scrubs that were covered in blood. She saw the three and the two dogs and went to scream.

PFFT!

Yvette popped her right in the throat, dropping her to the floor. The woman grasped at her throat as it gushed blood. Her eyes went wide in shock as a simple trip to go get some water, had turned into the last five minutes of her life.

They advanced, coming to a stop where the woman had come from. Michaels noticed a window was above their heads. While Yvette and Julie stayed crouched low, he raised up and was able to catch a glimpse of a team of medical staff... extracting parts from a female.

He grinded his teeth in anger. Seeing red, Michaels rose all the way up and pointed his gun at the window.

Yvette and Julie shot up and took aim at the crew alongside their lieutenant. The medical staff saw them and screamed in fear.

Yvette, Julie, and Michaels started dumping, blowing through the glass. The doctor's head exploded. Two nurses caught hot ones in their faces. Another member of the team was lifted up and tossed back into the wall when Yvette and Julie blasted him at the same time.

BOC! BOC! BOC! BOC! BOC! BOC!

"Aaaahhhh, fuuck!"

Yvette and Julie heard the gunshots, but the second they heard Michaels howl in pain, time seemed to freeze.

They turned and saw him go down, His vest had deflected the bullets that would have obliterated his spine, but the two slugs that had hit him in the back of his thigh crumbled him.

They saw the shooter about twenty feet down the hall. Sir and Rock immediately took off as he dipped into the cut-way that they had not seen when they came from the garage.

Julie took off behind the dogs, enraged that they got caught slipping. Yvette ran to Michaels' side, panicking at how much he was bleeding.

"I'm okay! I'm alright! Just help me up!" he told her.

BOOM! BOOM! BOOM! BOOM!

BOC! BOC! BOC! BOC! BOC! BOC!

POW! POW! POW! POW! POW! POW!

"Julie!" Yvette screamed as she and Michaels heard the gunfire coming from where she had run off to with Sir and Rock.

BRRRRRR! BRRRRRR! BRRRRRR!

They both heard Julie's AR firing then. They knew she had to be okay, at least enough to shoot an assault rifle.

"Let's go!" Michaels yelled and attempted to go help Julie.

"Wait! You're bleeding too much!" Yvette hollered back, stopping him.

As fast as she could, she ripped her shirt and tied his leg off above the two wounds, hoping it would drastically slow the bleeding.

They crept off then, rushing to get to Julie. They burst through a set of doors that led to a massive supply room. Bullets flew the second they entered.

Yvette and Lieutenant Michaels dropped down as a barrage flew in their direction.

"Stay down!"

They heard Julie's voice just then. Scrambling towards where a few big wooden crates were stacked up, they ducked behind them, taking cover.

The sounds of Sir and Rock barking mixed in with the gunshots. Yvette checked on Michaels, then she searched for Julie. Bullets continued flying in every direction. Smoke had started filling the room. Yvette remembered seeing a few boxes and bottles on metal shelves with hazardous material stickers on them... the type that exploded when the heat from fire got too close.

Yvette saw a man make a run for it. She pointed her gun to hit him up, but Sir and Rock beat her to it.

She saw three others hop out from their hiding spots, then try to run for the door as the fire inside grew.

Yvette pointed at one and popped him in his left temple. Julie hopped up from her hiding place with her hunting knife just then. She ran and jumped on one of the remaining two, taking him to the ground, then she stabbed him square in the face.

Michaels shot up and took the third guy out with a headshot, putting one right through the center of his forehead.

Julie went berserk. She stabbed the man's face repeatedly, not giving a fuck about blood splashing up in her face. She blacked out, pissed, stuck in a killing frenzy, stabbing and jabbing, screaming like a wild animal.

"JuJu!"

Yvette yelled her name.

"Tran!" Michaels yelled, as Julie continued jabbing the way-past-dead man's face.

They grabbed Julie, right as Sir and Rock delivered their target to the afterlife. Julie blinked as Yvette and Michaels dragged her away from the annihilated corpse, pulling her out of the burning room. Yvette yelled for Sir and Rock. The dogs ran to catch up with them all.

They got up out of the room just as something exploded inside, setting off a chain reaction of explosions. Hurrying away from the raging fire, the two carried a stoic Julie back to the van. Lieutenant Sikes was just making it back, with his shotgun in hand, Ranger at his side, and two naked men in front of him, trembling in fear.

He saw Michaels had been wounded but seemed to be okay. Julie was covered in blood like someone took a water gun that was filled with red paint and drenched her. Sir and Rock both had bloody muzzles but were fine.

"I'd give anything to go through whatever you all did, if it could erase from my mind what I walked in on," Sikes said to them, catching a chill up his spine as he glanced at the Greek men.

Another explosion rocked the building just then. As fast as they could, they got the organ-trafficker boss and his bitch into the van and hopped in, then Sikes mashed the gas pedal to the floor, launching them forward, blasting through the garage door and speeding away as more explosions went off, flames quickly engulfed the whole building within minutes.

***

The two ladies sat in the BMW, parked across from the burning building. They saw the van blow through the garage door and get ghost, a minute or so before the whole place went up.

Samantha shook her head.

Bernice chuckled. "Your husband's not gonna' be happy," she told Samantha.

Starting her engine, Samantha put it in drive and pulled off, grumbling angrily under her breath.

***

The Greeks were dropped off at the spot with all the others that Yvette, Julie, and their bosses had rounded up for the two ladies, then Sikes shot straight to the hospital for Michael's gunshot wounds to be treated.

The doctor assured them all that the lieutenant would be fine, with rest and recuperation.

Thankful, Yvette and Julie went outside to check on the dogs. Yvette's phone rang. She pulled it from the side pocket of her black combat cargo pants and saw it was T.G.

"Hey, baby," she said, happy to get a call from him, but still shaken by how things could've gone a whole lot worse.

When he spoke, she heard the urgency in his voice. Yvette nudged Julie and put it on speaker phone. Their eyes went wide at the same exact time.

"We're on the way! Don't lose them!" Yvette told him, then she ended the call.

Hopping into the van, Julie got behind the wheel and started the engine, slamming it into drive. Yvette shot Sikes a quick text, then grabbed her AR, ejecting the spent clip, and slapping in a fresh one, then did the same for Julie's, as Julie blew up out of the ER's exit with the strobes flashing and the siren wailing loudly.

Chapter 13

"Nigga, I don't give a mother fuck about them broke-ass, hurtin'-ass, peon-ass niggas! If a muhfucka think they finna move coke out in my hood and not kick up a piece of that, 'erybody gon' die! Fuck the bullshit! On Nation, folks!"

Milo was heated. He hadn't wanted to put the young coke boy to sleep, nor had he wanted to put hot ones in the others he had been with, but he wasn't raised to let debts go uncollected. The penalty for moving anything in his neighborhood, be it coke, dope, pills, or pussy, Milo wanted a piece of it, non-negotiable.

After a call from his guys came in, telling him that some dude came to the hood and dropped off a lot of cocaine, shit that was so pure that even a few of his own guys got to jumping ship to climb aboard the opposition's vessel. He immediately called up his right-hand man Eagle, hopped into his new Rolls-Royce Phantom, then went to scoop his homie up.

Eagle had two gorgeous Brazilian women with him. They were way more than just pretty faces and good pussy. All of them strapped, they shot north from Chicago, out to Waukegan. Forty minutes later, Milo pulled up to a house by the corner of South Park and Water Street, where there were seven young and wild Maniac Latin Disciples, posted outside of the house's fence.

With the Lake County Sheriff's station and Lake County Jail literally fifteen seconds away in downtown Wauk-Town in Milo's mind, he screwed a silencer into the barrel of his Glock 9mm.

Eagle and the two female goons got out with their own silenced thumpers and followed Milo to the group of Latin Folks.

The shot-caller of the mob led Milo and his people into the house, down to the basement, where the four dope boys were being held captive by the Maniacs.

***

"Aye, lil' niggas. Y'all must think comin' into another man's hood, 'n dumpin' yayo on his streets is acceptable, huh?" Milo said, gun in his right hand, left hand over his right hand, standing in front of the one the shorty 'Yacs declared to be the lead man.

"Man, we just tryna' get a few dollars, fam. It ain't 'een that serious for all this," said Twist, an eighteen-year-old Black kid with long black and red-tipped dreadlocks in fresh two-strand twists, dripping in icy jewelry and rocking Amiri with the high-top Amiri sneakers.

Milo looked over at his guys that were in the opposite corner, the ones attempting to buy the competition's yayo. The three were being held against their will by the two older Maniacs, with sawed-off shotguns.

"Take them lil' dumbass niggas outside in the back and put 'em on the wall. Each of 'em got a minute, head to toe," Milo ordered, issuing a beat-down violation, though the youngsters had done nothing to violate a single code in the Nation's laws.

The three were escorted out to get violated. Milo looked at the half-brick of powder cocaine sitting on the table off to the side, and the pistols that had switches on them, laying next to the yayo, taken from Twist and his guys.

"A half-brick is more than a few dollars, my nigga'," Milo told Twist, and raised his gun up, pointing it right at the youngster's face.

Twist refused to show weakness, especially in front of his guys.

"On Vice Lord, do what 'chu gotta do, fam! Ain't no—"

PFFT!

Milo put a slug through Twist's left eye. His brains exploded out the back of his head, splashing in the faces of his Lord brothers behind.

Twist's body fell backwards and hit the ground. Blood started pouring out of the gaping hole in his head. His guys all looked down at their mans, shocked speechless.

"I hate it when people say, 'Ain't no bitch in my blood, Joe'," Milo said.

He gave Eagle, Adrianna, and Caylee the word. The three raised their guns and dumped on the others but only shooting them where they wouldn't immediately die... if they didn't get help... fast!

Milo walked up to one of them and crouched down, looking into his glazed eyes as he bled from the holes in his legs.

"They call me Milo D, lil' nigga! This is my hood! I'm a muhfuckin' Maniac Latin Disciple! Tell whoever you work for to stay the fuck away from here, or next time, you all die!"

***

Eagle chuckled at how pissed Milo was. When it came to money, Milo didn't play any games. He respected that, though, he wasn't keen on killing kids.

"Nigga, chill out," he told Milo from the backseat. "You got a bad bitch next to you. We handled the 'biz, them clown-ass shorties gon' get some Band-Aids, go tell they big homie what happened, then we gon' lay 'em all out. Until then,"

Milo said with a pause, "aye, Adrianna, give my nigga some head so he can relax."

Milo didn't put up a fight in any way as the scantily clad Boricua got up on her knees in the seat, reached over to his crotch, and freed his hardening cock.

As he headed up to Glen Rock Street, making a left, Milo's eyes rolled to the back of his head when the girl took his dick into her mouth. He kept one hand on the steering wheel and reached the other around to feel on Adrianna's ass. It was so phat and juicy. He smacked it, then lifted the tiny leather skirt she had on, palming her bare ass cheeks. She had no panties on, nor a thong.

"Yeah, bitch, Mamame lo este cabron!" Milo groaned, approaching a red light at Glen Rock and Jackson Street.

In the back, Caylee was on her knees in front of Eagle, his dick out and both of her hands jerking him while she sucked.

"Ooohhh, sshit! Fuck!" Eagle cussed, as Caylee pleased the fuck out of him, so good that he had to squeeze his eyes closed.

Just then, the all-too-familiar sound of a police horn blared loudly. Both Milo and Eagle opened their eyes and saw red and blue lights flashing, filling the inside of Milo's Phantom.

"Shit!" Milo cursed, not sure if he should hit the gas and take the police on a high-speed or see what they did wrong.

Adrianna lifted her head and hurried to sit back in her seat. Caylee did the same. Milo and Eagle quickly tucked their dicks back in and zipped up their pants.

"Put the vehicle in park, shut the engine off, and step out of the car with your hands up!" they heard what sounded like a woman shout through a loudspeaker.

Deciding to comply, since neither of them had their dirty guns, and no drugs in the car, Milo, Adrianna, Eagle, and Caylee did as they were told, getting out of the Phantom with their hands up.

"Face away from my vehicle and get down on your knees! Move the wrong way, and you will be shot!"

Again, they obeyed. Milo muttered a curse under his breath. The first thing he planned on doing when he made it to the county was call his lawyer, for him and Eagle. The bitches were on their own, and likely to catch the murder charges when he blamed it on them.

WHAM!

Milo heard Caylee scream, then he heard his homie shout in panic. He turned his head just as Adrianna caught a blunt object to the back of her head, sending her face down, right as a black bag was put over his head.

"Aye! What the—"

CRACK!

In the dark, he saw stars when something bashed him on the side of the head. Dazed, Milo felt himself being cuffed, then yanked up off the ground. He was dragged a short distance, then felt himself get into a vehicle. A second later, he heard a growling, really close to him.

***

"You're sexy when you play bad-cop, baby," T.G. said, after he threw Milo into the van.

Yvette giggled. "Awww! Thank you, my king, but ain't nobody playin'."

Bucks tossed Milo's homie in next to him. Sir, Rock, and Ranger growled as the two Puerto Ricans squirmed around, panicking and whimpering.

"Let's get goin'," Julie said, coming back from putting the two girls in the trunk of the Phantom.

"You two go ahead. Bro and I gotta slide back over to see them lil' 'Yac niggas," T.G. said. "We'll meet you there."

He kissed his woman on the lips and patted her ass. Bucks kissed his girl, then as Yvette got behind the wheel in the van, and Julie behind the Rolls-Royce's wheel, T.G. and

Bucks jumped into the all-black Dodge Charger SRT-8, dipping towards Southpark to finish up.

***

"On the D! We all finna get hit wit' so much coke for doin' that for Milo, Joe!" Lil' Wacko exclaimed, geeked to have handled some business for their big dog.

"Nation, folks! When we get good, we finna move on all them bitch ass Kings and take over 8th Street!" another one of the MLDs called Nero declared.

Lil' Wacko, Nio, Leak, and Tip stood out in front of the house, passing a blunt of Candy Haze back and forth, while a few others and a group of Nation hoes were up on the porch, blazing loud, sipping liquor, while some Latin trap music boomed from inside of the house.

A loud engine, unmistakably a Hemi roared up the road to their left.

They looked towards where South Park and Water Street intersects. A Black Charger hit a right turn onto their block and came fast.

The youngsters all went for their guns to up and dump on the unknown vehicle. They guys up on the porch did the same, while their bitches ducked for cover.

The Charger slid to a stop in front of the Maniacs. Lil' Wacko and his guys pointed their guns, ready to fire.

The passenger window rolled down a second later.

"Aye, Wacko! I need some weed, Joe!" Lil' Wacko heard the passenger shout.

He furrowed his brows. "Who dat?" he hollered back, lowering his gun.

"This Greedy G's cousin, fam! Mike Mike!"

"Oh, aight. I got chu', fam," he said.

The others lowered their guns then. Hearing the request for some stanky-bank made them relax. Lil' Wacko tucked his pistol, pulled out a Ziploc bag full of exotic, and walked towards the car.

"Aye, I ain't got shit bagged up. What chu' tryna get, fam?" he asked, trying to see inside the dark car.

The second he got to within five feet of the car, a large barrel came out of the window. Lil' Wacko froze in fear when he saw it.

"Say hello to this big bitch, you little bitch!" he heard the man in the passenger seat shout.

T.G. pulled the trigger and flames shot out of the barrel, nearly thirty feet long. He roasted the young gangbanger and caught the other as he swept from left to right.

Bucks hopped out and hurled concussion grenades at the ones on the porch. They didn't get a chance to squeeze off a single shot before the first grenade exploded, disorienting them all. The second and third went into the second floor's open windows, hitting the people that were inside.

T.G. hopped out and ran past the human fireballs, screaming in agony as they burned. He ran up on the ones on the porch and torched them. Bucks, with his Draco, followed him inside the house, where he pointed and fired up everything he could.

One of the people that had been upstairs, hit by the concussion grenade blast, jumped down the stairs, attempting to flee.

BRRRRRRRRRRRR!

Bucks caught him before he made it out. One tug of the trigger was all it took. The man was cut in half by the quick burst of 7.62mm rounds.

The fire quickly started spreading. T.G. let up off the trigger. He and Bucks ran out of the house towards the car. Bucks saw two more guys trying to run, after they had bravely jumped out of the upstairs window.

Bucks ran up on them and popped them up, dropping them just feet away from their homies.

"Let's bounce!" T.G. said, heading back towards the whip.

Bucks ran and hopped back behind the wheel, slamming it into drive and floored it, speeding from the fiery massacre before a single police siren had even started wailing.

***

An Hour Later...

Yvette opened her gloved hand and blew the tiny particles right into Milo's eyes.

"Aaaaaaaaaaagggggggghhhhhhh!" he screamed, in excruciating pain from the crushed glass cutting his eyeballs.

Eagles' eyes were on fire from the liquid habanero pepper-ammonia mixture that Julie squirted into his eyes.

The two cried in agony. Yvette, Julie and the dogs all watched Milo and Eagle writhing in pain on the floor of the tall, abandoned building they were on top of. Milo and Eagle had no clue where they were, all they had seen when the bags came off their heads was a pitch-black sky, with only a few stars in it.

"That shit gots to hurt," Yvette said.

"Not enough," Julie added.

She pulled a handcuff key from her pocket, then Yvette muscled Milo onto his stomach. Julie uncuffed him, then Eagle.

"Both of y'all shut the fuck up and get up!" Yvette demanded.

Though in sheer agony, the two stood, blind as men with no eyes at all.

"You get one chance to walk off on this," Yvette said. "Go! March! Or I will shoot you both in y'all's balls!"

Julie did everything she could to keep from laughing her ass off as the blind guys tried to find their exit, hands out in front of them, searching for a wall or a door. Yvette bit her bottom lip, trying not to laugh herself.

"Hurry up and get out before I release the dogs!" Yvette yelled.

Julie picked up a rock and hurled it, hitting Milo in the back of his head.

Milo took off running blindly, not caring if he ran into something. He ran full speed in a straight line, until his feet left the solid surface, and he suddenly started falling.

***

T.G. hopped out of the Charger. Bucks got out after him. They heard screaming, coming from above.

SMASH!

The roof of the car crushed in like a giant stomped on it. They both jumped back in shock. They saw the man on the car, dead, leaking blood.

"Oh, shit... is that—"

SMACK!

A loud thump came from behind him. T.G. jumped back, upping his pistol. When he saw Eagle lying splayed out on the ground, his eyes went wide.

Bucks looked up and saw the movement of two figures.

"Bae?" he heard Julie holler.

"Yeah! It's me! I think you dropped somethin'!" Bucks yelled back.

"Sorry, Bucks! We'll buy you a new one!" Yvette then hollered, which made T.G. bust out laughing.

"You good, sis! I stole it!"

"Oh... okay! Hii, baby!" she then shouted to T.G.

"Heey, sexy! Wit' cho' thick ass! Bring y'all asses on! We hungry as fuck, Joe!" T.G. hollered up.

"Okay! Be right down!"

T.G. and Bucks then looked at the dead guys, then exchanged glances with each other.

"What a life we live, my nigga," Bucks said, chuckling to himself.

"Wouldn't trade it for the world, bro," T.G. replied, loving how crazy shit got, and how he, his brother from another mother, and the two baddest bitches on earth always got through the hurdles that the street life tossed at them.

Chapter 14

Two Months Later...

Summer faded. Fall had arrived. The days were a little shorter. T.G. and Bucks had the whole Illinois region supplied.

All two hundred bricks were gone. The white turned into green, lots of it. More money than Bucks, T.G., Yvette, and Julie had ever seen in their lives. They were taking over one city at a time. Recruiting soldiers that were always ready for war, hungry hustlers, blood-thirsty killers. With the help and expertise of Javi, his wife, Macho, and his ladies, Bucks and T.G. made some very wise investments, and were taught how to hide how they got such large sums of money to build such prestigious businesses.

Yvette and Julie, after completing the job set forth by Samantha and Bernice, got their lieutenants, their men, and themselves, out of hot water. The heat was gone, and they were back to their regular lives as they knew them.

Now recruited into the K9 unit under Sikes, the two had also been promoted. Yvette and Julie were now Sergeant Jones and Sergeant Tran. A week after their promotions, they were out in charge of a team of ladies, freshly joining the K9 unit, still getting to the things their ridiculously expensive dogs could do.

What bothered Yvette and Julie, was the fact that Webster had vanished without a trace. Even the Valdez family couldn't find him, which told them one thing… he had some serious help.

Reuben had gone back to Colombia, likely to lay low. Many of his soldiers and shooters had been dropped into shallow graves, or taken and dismembered, or stuffed into drums full of acid and burned, never to be seen again.

***

Bucks cruised in his silver 2021 Ferrari SF90 Stradale that ran him nearly half a million dollars, heading to where the exotic and foreign auto dealership/customization shop was, out in the Lake Forest area. He hopped off Route 41, matching the words to 21 Savage's verse in Usher's new hit song, making his way to what used to be a big Mercedes-Benz dealership, but was now B&T Auto Imports.

Turning in, he couldn't help but smile at the big lot filled with what belonged to the previous owners, plus all the foreigns and exotic hyper cars that Bucks and T.G. had managed to score contracts with the manufacturers, personally, to sell their vehicles. The relationship they had so suddenly formed with Javi and his family proved to be way more beneficial than either of them could have imagined.

He parked his 'Rarri in the spot with his name on it and hopped out. Entering the glass, gold, and marble structure, Bucks was greeted emphatically by every one of his employees as he headed to the inner service area.

Inside the long section, where more vehicles were parked, a custom-painted eighteen-wheeler had been backed in. Bucks went around the sleek green and gold big rig, passing the NASCAR-style enclosed car transport trailer, with Valdez Auto Transport, LLC decaled on the side.

At the driver's door of the brand new Peterbilt 589, Bucks knocked and waited. The sounds of Doja Cat's "97" flowed through the open window. He heard a pig squeal, then a second later, Evelyn Valdez appeared.

"Okay, then! Mirate tu, papi!" Evelyn had a big smile. "Looking all GQ handsome 'n shit!"

Bucks did a quick pose for her, showing off his custom-tailored Tom Ford suit, with the leather dress shoes to match. Diamonds sparkled in his ear, his hair cut in a fresh bald fade with the waves spinning out of control up on top, beard lined up sharply. He sported a custom, Cartier diamond watch on his wrist and had on a diamond pinkie ring.

"Yeah. A nigga lookin' fly, right?" he said, striking one more pose.

Evelyn chuckled, opening her door up. Her brown-furred, mini-potbellied pig squealed as she climbed out, dressed in a T-shirt with the company name across her breasts, leggings, and Jordan 12s on her feet.

Goddamn! Bucks thought, as so much ass became visible when Evelyn climbed down from her truck.

"You aight," Evelyn said, reaching up and cuffing her pig. "You might wanna' put somethin' shiny onto a woman's finger, while you pullin' up in million-dollar 'Rarris and flossin' out. Bitches be flockin' to any nigga that look like he got a few dollars and maybe, a nice body."

He laughed as she led him to the rear of her fifty-three-foot-long car-carrier. With the remote to it on her key chain, Evelyn unlocked the tailgate door, then worked the remote, lowering the tailgate down until it was level with the bottom rack.

"Hold my pig," she told him, handing Bucks her pig.

The mini pig was thrust into his arms. He squealed as if crying for his owner to come back. Bucks rubbed behind his ears and spoke softly to him, calming the pig's nerves while Evelyn stepped inside of the trailer to back out what was inside.

First came the white 2021 Ferrari F8 Spider with red interior on black rims, then a gray and black 2014 Bugatti

Veyron Vitesse edition, along with a gun-metal gray 2020 Lamborghini Aventador SVJ Spyder then last, a vintage 1967 Pontiac GTO, fully restored to original form.

Evelyn parked them in a row. Bucks joined her at the front of the Bugatti. She popped the hood and revealed not a sixteen-cylinder twin-turbo engine, but thirty kilos of pure cocaine. Thirty more were in the other two cars' front ends, and in the GTO'S big deep trunk, a hundred and ten more bricks, bringing the total back to two hundred bricks.

Javi and his cousins were more than sure that Bucks and T.G. could handle more, but, respectfully, they declined, not wanting to go but so big, since they were doing exceedingly well already. Greed sank ships just like loose lips. They had all seen it firsthand.

Evelyn exchanged the keys to the cars for her pig. She got back into the truck and started the powerful Cummins engine under the hood. Bucks let her out and watched as the beautiful young Dominican maneuvered the long tractor-trailer out of his dealership.

Just as he took in a deep breath of cool air, Julie pulled up in her brand-new Bentley Flying Spur, looking fly as hell herself with her sassy Chanel shades on, with Rock riding shotgun.

Bucks smiled. He stood back as she pulled inside. She went and parked next to the GTO and killed the engine. Bucks closed the garage and went to her.

Dressed in a pin-striped Valentino skirt-suit, Julie was looking like a boss. It matched the dark-blue color of her Bentley, with the exclusive white interior matching the pinstripes running horizontally on it. Bucks bit his bottom lip. She was also wearing dark-blue panty hose that accentuated her sexy legs. A white leather belt with a "V" belt buckle, and white Valentino six-inch pumps on her feet completed her look.

Her hair was in a sophisticated bun. Vintage pearl jewelry in her ears, around her neck, and on her wrist, a stainless-steel Tiffany & Co edition Patek Philippe Nautilus. She smelled like strawberries, and it made Bucks' mouth water.

"Well, someone's enjoyin' ridin' around lookin' good as fuck, in her new whip," Bucks said, as Rock ran up to him, wagging his fluffy tail excitedly.

Julie walked right up to him, grabbed him by his shirt, and pulled him in between her car and the GTO.

Without a word, while looking up into his eyes, Julie undid and dropped his pants and his Tom Ford boxer briefs. She freed his dick, wrapping a hand around it, as it began hardening. Bucks loved it when his woman pulled surprise oral attacks on him. He was glad none of the mechanics were in yet.

Julie sank down to her knees and started kissing and licking all over his dick. She ran her tongue along the side, down to his balls. She held his cock upwards, out of her way, and started licking his nuts.

Bucks groaned, cursing as he felt her tongue making circles. He leaned back against the GTO and relished in the feeling of his dick going in and out of her warm mouth.

He looked down, watching her glossy dark-blue lips wrapped around his shaft. He felt her cupping his balls, massaging them. His eyes rolled to the back of his head. A few minutes later, he felt his nut rising.

Julie started jerking him while she sucked, moaning and humming, sending deep vibrations through his loins. She heard him groaning. She felt him trembling. His cock spasmed in her mouth, then seconds later, while he fucked her face, making his balls smack against her chin, Bucks exploded in her mouth. Julie swallowed every last drop of his cum, then licked her lips clean of him.

"Whoa," he said, taking a deep breath against the ol' school muscle car. "That was… maaaan, you be tryna' make a nigga lose brain cells the way you be suckin' on this muhfucka."

Julie busted out laughing. She took his hand and was helped up from her knees.

"Weeell... it is your birthday, baby," she told him, fixing his clothes back, and smoothing his suit jacket out. "You are handsome, smart, ambitious, and so gangsta that it makes my pussy drip every time I see a gun in your hand. You deserve to get that big dick sucked whenever you want, and I will gladly let you fuck my face anywhere we go."

Bucks again found himself stuck in true awe of his woman. She was the shit. Period.

"Wow. I am the luckiest man on earth to have you as my woman," he told her.

Julie cheesed up, blushing hard at his words.

"But," he continued. "I don't want you to be my woman anymore, Julie."

Her face fell then.

"What?"

Bucks started smiling. "I want you to be more than just my woman, bae."

"What are you talkin' about, Bernard? I'm 'bout to smack yo' ass if you break up with me!"

"Naw, Julie. I'm not breakin' up with you, my love," he assured her. Bucks dug down into his pocket and pulled something out. The second he started sinking down to one knee, Julie screamed in shock. She screamed again when she saw the big flawless diamond ring in the box. Surrounded by diamond baguettes, with a big centralized oval ruby, the Harry Winston ring was unique in design, and cost more than the average working individual's yearly salary. "I'm tryin' to give you my last name, bae," Bucks continued.

Tears filled Julie's eyes as the moment actually hit her. Her dream was coming true.

Rock trotted over and sat next to the gobsmacked Asian, tail wagging, sensing the excitement she was feeling.

"Julie Tran, will you marry me, and make me the happiest Black man to ever have lived?"

She winked away a few tears as she gazed down into his eyes. They were so full of love and passion.

"Only if you promise to keep making me the happiest Vietnamese woman to ever have lived," Julie replied through her tears.

Bucks smiled. "I promise, baby. I love you more than I will ever be able to describe with words. So, I will show you, every day, for the rest of my life, if you will let me."

Julie smiled then. She started nodding her head.

"Yes, Bernard. Yes, baby. Yes. Yes! Yes! Yeess!" she cried, as her emotions went into overdrive as the realization that she was going to be his wife hit her right at that moment. "I will! I will marry you, Bernard! I'm yours, and you are mines, for the rest of our lives."

Bucks' own eyes welled with tears of joy. He took the ring out of the box, slid it onto her finger, and stood. He kissed her lips, cupping her face gently, with both of his hands. She could feel his love, transferring from his lips to hers as if he was a battery, supplying her with power to function. He pulled back after a minute and touched her belly.

"I'm gonna' be a father, a husband to the most beautiful woman in the world."

Rock barked three times at them, standing up, tail still wagging a hundred miles an hour.

"And we already got a dog," Bucks added, patting his leg for Rock to join them.

Julie gushed vibrantly. "We got it all, baby. Now let's go get some more."

Bucks handed her the key to the GTO that he'd had in his pocket. He put her behind the wheel, got Rock in the back. Hopping in next to his woman, the ol' school shook when Julie started the monstrous engine up. She put it in drive, pulled out of the garage, and headed for the highway.

With more than a hundred birds in the trunk, a trainer killer in the back seat, and a bad bitch with a gun driving, Bucks reclined his seat and thought about a few more large-scale moves he had been wanting to make, with his fiancée right at his side.

***

Tears fell from her eyes as the pain in her chest made her feel like someone was literally squeezing her heart. She couldn't believe what she was seeing. No way was it possible. She blinked her eyes, wiping away the tears, thinking that they were making her see things. She even replayed the video clip three times, praying she was tripping, and wasn't seeing the foulness on the live video feed alert that had popped up on her iPhone while assisting a young woman, with two kids, and bruises on her arms and face, get registered and settled into the Women's Safe Haven that she and her homegirl started.

How could he do this to me? I been so good to him! Yvette thought, as she watched T.G. engaging in a threesome, in the guest house of their new mansion.

She was shocked. Had he not realized that there were motion-activated cameras all around the house? And in every building on the one point eight acres of land they lived on?

Yvette couldn't tell who the women were. She could only see that one was dark skinned, while the other was a few shades lighter. From how the camera was positioned, in the ceiling of the opened-up lounge area, Yvette could see her man, fucking the dark-skinned chick from the back, while she ate the other chick's pussy, who sat on the couch with her legs up and wide open. The audio capability allowed Yvette to hear the sounds of skin smacking, T.G. groaning, and the women moaning.

Knocking at the door took her attention away from the screen. She paused the video and hollered for who it was to give her a second.

Yvette hurried to wipe her face, then she took a few deep breaths. Half a minute later, she stood, smoothing out her silk Versace button shirt, and fixing her Versace leather high-waist pencil skirt.

She walked around her desk, her Jimmy Choo pumps' heels clicking loudly on the marble floor in her deluxe first floor office. Opening the door, Yvette saw Alfonzo there, wearing casual attire, with a fresh haircut, neat beard. With him, was a girl that looked too young to be in a place as such. And she looked terrified.

"Hi," Yvette said to the little girl, whom she could tell was of mixed ethnicities easily. "I'm Yvette Jones, what's your name?"

The little girl's eyes stayed looking down towards the floor. Yvette's heart broke. She looked so scared and precious at the same time, in a little denim jean and jacket suit with a superstar T-shirt, her sandy-brown hair in two pigtails, and her little Nikes on her feet.

"She's been silent since I went to pick her up from Child Services," Alfonzo told Yvette. He crouched down next to the girl. "Yonnie, this lady is very nice, and very fun, you don't have to be scared. I promise, you will like her," he said to the little girl, then he looked at Yvette, with a smile. "Just like I do," he added.

Yvette tried hard not to smile, but ever since she had met Alfonzo, he had her eye, and she had his. He was tall, dark, handsome and athletic. She could hear it in the way that he spoke in proper ways that he wasn't from the hood, but she could sense that deep inside, he had it in him. A bad boy in nice clothes had always been intriguing to her, as it had been with plenty of other women.

***

Yvette was about to get Yonnie to go with her. She spent a few hours with the seven-year-old. Yonnie started opening up when Yvette discovered that Oreos were Yonnie's favorite snack. They both munched on America's favorite cookie and sipped apple juice. Things got better when Sir decided to come in from the yard outside of Yvette's office. Yonnie fell for him right away, lighting up like a kid getting their first pile of change from the Tooth Fairy.

Yvette's iPhone rang as Yonnie played with Sir. She saw T.G.'s name on the screen and sent him right to voicemail. A minute later, he sent her a text.

You coming home tonight?

Yvette didn't answer. She put her phone in her bag and called one of her employees. In a matter of minutes, Delilah entered.

"Yonnie, this is Delilah. She's nice just like me. She's going to show you the prettiest bedroom ever. Is that okay with you?"

"Can you go with me?" Yonnie asked, in her tiny little angelic voice that would make even the most hardened gangster's heart swell.

Yvette smiled and nodded. "Of course, princess. Let's all go together."

***

After she and Delilah took Yonnie to the luxurious bedroom, set up for a child aged five to ten, the ladies and Sir stayed with Yonnie to make sure she was comfortable. Having opened the center just over a month ago, Yvette split her time from her job, to training to become a counselor for women, young, and old, along with tender-aged children. She had gotten government funding to help, but also used money Javi's wife had shown her and Julie how to use for something that was heavily watched by the law and would not get put under the scope.

Yonnie was there while her drug-dealing parents battled for their lives in the court of law. Temporary loss of custody was standard, and it made Yonnie have to be without her mother and father, until God knows when. But, until there was an outcome, Yvette planned to be there for Yonnie, just as she had been for the five other children, that unfortunately, had to be adopted out, since their parents wanted to live on the wrong side of the law, and not consider their children's lives being put at risk because of it.

***

Sir had grown an instant bond with Yonnie, so Yvette opted to let him stay with the little girl overnight. The night shift employees and security, who were off-duty Illinois State Police Officers in Yvette's and Julie's department, all arrived on time and assumed their posts. Yvette waited until Yonnie was fast asleep, with Sir laid out next to her, before she left out.

Torn up about Yonnie's predicament, and the man she loved cheating on her, with whores in their home, Yvette found it very difficult to not cry when she went to get her purse from her office. She took a deep breath, then with the key fob to her 2021 Aston Martin DBX truck, Yvette left her office.

***

"Miss Jones! Hey! Miss Jones!"

Yvette heard her name being called as she remote-started her engine. Turning around, she saw Alfonzo was hollering at her, from over by his early 2000 Mercedes-Benz S500. When he saw he had her attention, he ran over to her.

"What's up, 'Fonz?" she said to him, trying to keep from looking at him in a lustful way. "Everything aight?"

"Yeah, I was just… uh… wondering, if you didn't have any plans for the evening, maybe you could join me for dinner?" he asked, nervously.

Yvette felt her lips curl up into a smile without even meaning to. He had attempted to ask her out a few times before, but she hadn't been anywhere near wanting to entertain another man. But now, why not? Her man was fucking hoes in their guest house. Why shouldn't she go out with a decent dude with a good head on his shoulders, with lips that made Yvette fantasize some extremely naughty things in her mind.

"Come on," Alfonzo nearly pleaded with that smile that made Yvette's nipples harden.

"Maybe. Where you takin' me?" she then asked, giving him the most flirtatious smile.

She could immediately see how he was trying so hard to contain his excitement. It made her want to laugh, but she refrained from doing so.

"There's a new spot in Vernon Hills that's a mix of an Italian restaurant/winery, and a sports car exhibit."

"Oh yeah? That sounds dope. Okay." Yvette hit the unlock button on her idling Aston Martin truck. "I'll drive."

"Sounds good to me, Miss Jones. I—"

"Uh-uh. I'm not sure why you think I wanna' be called that, but my name is Yvette. You three years younger than me, not ten or twenty."

"Okay, then, Yvette." Alfonzo gave her that smile again. This time she felt that sweet spot that was between her legs get a little moist. He opened her door for her and took her hand. "After you, beautiful."

Yvette did everything she could to keep from blushing, but the man had her lightweight swooning. She got up into her SUV and settled into the lavish five-seater. Alfonzo closed the door, hopped in on the other side, and awed at how dope her ride was.

"If being a cop affords someone a ride like this these days, maybe I should sign up for the academy," Alfonzo said, buckling himself in.

Yvette chuckled. "Be careful what you desire. Anything worth having, best believe, 'Fonz, it came from blood, sweat, and tears, lots of it," she told him, pulling off from where she was parked.

"I hear that, Yvette," he said, then told her where the eatery he wanted to go was.

***

Watching through the windshield of her BMW, Samantha remained with a poker-face mug, though inside, she was boiling.

"You know, you actually look like you might hate her more than I do."

Samantha turned and looked at the man she had secretly married, who never wore his wedding ring. The sight of his sarcastic smirk pissed her off even more.

"What I hate, is beyond her, you slimy womanizing son of a bitch." She put her car in drive and pulled off. "With a limp dick," she added.

"Hey! I have Viagra, Sammie. You know how good it works!"

"Haa! Works for you, Dale. A hard dick means nothing if it can't bring a woman to an orgasm. Maybe that's why Jones refused your played-out advances towards her!"

He shook his head as her word bruised his ego. "Whatever, Samantha! At least I'm not sleeping with five different guys in my squad!"

At least they all give me multiple orgasms! she thought, right as her new target's face popped into her head.

Samantha planned to put her new plan of action into play, as soon as she got rid of her husband for the evening. She knew exactly where her mark was going to be.

Chapter 15

"You got me all the way fucked up. I told you that since you buyin' all of 'em, I'll dump on you for ten thousand a brick. That means I need one point one million, fam... not nine hundred eighty-five thousand! Where the fuck is my money?" Bucks snapped, glaring at the French gun-dealer angrily.

Julie stood silently next to her fiancé. Rock was in the car, his protective instincts locked in, sensing the anger in Julie and in Bucks, though he couldn't see them.

"I apologize, my friend," said Pierre, with a sly smile on his pasty-white face. "There must be some confusion. I am very sure I counted the amount requested."

Julie loathed the way he talked, and how every single word that came out of his mouth seemed to exude sarcasm.

"However," the French man continued. "It is not a problem to fix the issue."

In a big business meeting room in Pierre's estate, out in Palatine, Bucks and Julie had delivered one hundred and ten kilos of cocaine to the rich clothing designer, who was known for hosting the most extravagant events, all over the world. He was also said to be a cheap skate that hated paying for anything, though he was a very wealthy man.

With Pierre, were just two men. They looked pissed, and not necessarily because of Bucks and Julie. They were sure it had to do with the flamboyantly vibrant suits they wore that not many husky and muscular men should have on.

They both had MP5s in their hands, pointing down at the shiny veined marble floor… for the moment.

"Well, let's fix it then, my man. I have other business meetings to be at," Bucks told him, not once faltering.

Pierre nodded his head. He turned to one of his men and spoke in French.

"Tuez-les et tuez leur chien, puis prenez la cocaine."

Julie gasped, startling Bucks. The two men raised their guns and pointed at Bucks and Julie.

Immediately, Julie pushed her man out of the way, hard enough to send him to the floor. The shooters squeezed when Pierre yelled for them to kill Bucks and Julie, as he had done in French, along with the order to kill the dog, and take the coke.

"Bae!" Bucks yelled as bullets started flying.

Julie, hidden by the big oval table, was shielded by the gunfire. Bucks was tucked behind a big wooden desk to the side. Pierre yelled for his men to get them.

Julie stayed where she was, slipping her right hand into the waistline of her skirt. Able to see Bucks from where they both were, he mouthed to her, "Stay down!"

She mouthed back, "No! Fuck that!"

"Do not hide, people!" Pierre hollered. "There is no way out!"

Julie's eyes went to the floor. Her cop survival instincts kicked in. Down towards the other end of the room, she could see one of the men, creeping towards her, with both hands gripping his gun.

She glanced over at Bucks, catching his attention. She mouthed more words to him. He nodded his head and prepared to get his future wife and unborn child the hell up out of there.

"What are you waiting fooor?" Pierre shouted, standing behind the chair he had been sitting in. "Kill them! Hurry up, Pip! Get that bitch! Arturo! Get him!"

Pip, the bigger and brawnier of the two, could see a glint of her reflection on the shiny floor. He smiled evilly as he envisioned seeing her head explode when he put bullets through her brain.

Arturo, bringing up the other side of the table, side-stepped to his left, gun up, ready to fire the second he saw the Black man.

Pip neared where the woman was. He got ready to pivot and pop her, when just then, a balled-up piece of paper flew at him, from where the man ducked.

Pip's eyes averted to it, taking them off of her. In the split second that he looked away, the girl hopped up and hurled a razor-sharp knife, right at his face.

Arturo saw the girl shoot up from where she had hidden and launch the knife at his partner. Pip dropped to the floor, dead the second the blade shot through his right eye from her spot-on aim.

"No!" Pierre shouted, seeing the horrendous act.

Arturo went to fire at her before she could drop back out of his line of sight, but then, the man she had come with hopped up and hurled a stapler at his head.

CRACK!

He screamed in pain when the stapler opened up a gaping wound at his left temple. He dropped his gun, crying in agony, cupping his face as he bled profusely.

Pierre ran and dove for the gun. He had just picked it up when the Asian woman came flying at him. She jumped on him, grabbing his wrists and muscling them to the floor.

Shots fired as his finger squeezed the trigger. He tried to bring the gun down to shoot her, but she was waaay stronger than he looked.

Bucks ran up and delivered a field-goal kick to Pierre's crotch. He squealed like a terrified pig. Bucks pulled Julie off of him, and together, they watched him ball up into a fetal position, crying his eyes out while he squeezed a hand between his legs, holding his throbbing balls.

"Stupid bitch!" Julie spat, back up on her feet.

"Embrasse mon cul!" Pierre yelled.

"Kiss your ass, huh?" Julie grabbed Pip's gun while Bucks went and snatched up Arturo from the floor. "I do understand French, bitch! Now how 'bout you kiss these hot ones!"

BRRRRRR! BRRRRR! BRRRRRRR!

Bucks watched his fiancée make the French man's body jump from all the rounds she dumped into his chest and stomach. He faced Arturo to watch with him.

"You see that? Huh? Take a good look at yo' bitch ass boss. The punk-ass bitch that has you in that pink-ass suit! Take a good look at dude with the knife in his eye!" Bucks demanded, holding Arturo's head so that the man had no choice but to look.

Julie walked up to them, with pure demon in her eyes. Bucks let his head go. She smacked the shit out of Arturo with the gun, knocking a few teeth out of his mouth. He flew to the ground, bleeding heavily from his mouth.

"Ooohhooooweee! Daayyuuum! My girl a muhfuckin' gangsta!" Bucks exclaimed, geeked all the way up. Aye famo!" he said to the man. "Ya' know what the best part of havin' a lady that'll knock a bitch-ass clown like you out? I get to fuck her brains out when we get home! Woooo!"

Julie busted out laughing at her dude. "Crazy-ass man!"

"Check it out, though. This is what's gon' happen. You wanna' live through this? Make it home to fuck your bitch's brains out… or… whatever ya into?"

He nodded his head frantically.

"Aight. This what you gotta do. You gotta—"

BRRRRRRR!

Julie squeezed on the MPS's trigger and sent a stream of hot slugs into the man's face, blowing it inwards.

Bucks looked at her with puzzled brows.

"Y'all kill me with that prolonging shit, Joe! Fuck that! Get the money and we out! Simple!" she stated.

166

Bucks shook his head but couldn't help but smile. "My bitch so bad, lookin' waaay better than a bag of money, and she speaks French! Woo!"

***

"What the fuck? Why is this bitch not answerin' her phone?" growled T.G., after trying to call his woman again.

"You really gon' be mad about another bitch right after I just sucked yo' dick, again, for the third time in a row, though?" the thick, yellow-bone asked incredulously, still naked, on her knees in front of T.G. in the biggest bedroom of the guest bedroom.

T.G. heard her words. It struck a nerve like a person that was highly allergic to bees smacked a yellow jacket away from them.

SMACK!

Faster than he saw coming, T.G. delivered an open hand to her face, making her head snap to the right.

"Bitch! Get 'cho shit and get the fuck out!"

The dark-skinned girl walked back out from using the bathroom. She saw her friend scrambling to get her clothes, crying while she hurried about. She saw how red her face was, and how T.G. looked.

"Uh-uh! I know you didn't just lay yo' hands on her, dude!" Claire snapped, rushing over to Abbie.

"Yeah! I did, bitch! Both of y'all get the fuck outta my spot!" T.G. demanded, standing up and glaring at them menacingly.

They both hurried to get their underwear, bras, dresses, and their stilettos, which they had been wearing when T.G. ran into them at the club he had gone to dump off some coke. They were on him, as soon as he entered, and it was without a doubt that they were DTF and down for every nasty thing he wanted them to do.

"You gon' regret this, bitch ass nigga," the high yellow chick told him.

"Bitch, shut the fuck up and get out!"

Still naked, the ladies left out. T.G. threw his boxers on and watched them on the camera, making their way to where he had them park their car, out of sight, in case Yvette finally decided to come home.

He tried to resist the beautiful whores at the club. He really did, but he felt that Yvette was neglecting him, spending all her time at work, and at her and Julie's shelter. Julie spent almost all her time with Bucks. They were engaged from what he saw on the text he got from his homie earlier that day, and they were expecting a child. T.G. wanted that with his woman so badly, but she seemed to have pulled back, all when things felt like they couldn't get any better.

It was a blow to his heart. Yvette was his heart, and she was taking herself away from him, for some reason.

T.G. attempted to call her phone again. It went to voicemail this time.

He cursed, shaking his head. Then an idea popped into his mind.

"I'ma pop up on her," he said to himself, going into the GPS app that linked his phone, Yvette's, Julie's, and Bucks's, sharing their locations.

T.G. saw that she was in Vernon Hills, at some restaurant.

"What the hell?" he said to himself, with furrowed brows." This bitch can go out to eat, but can't answer my calls? Hell naw! On everything I love, let her be with a nigga… his ass is grass!"

T.G. hurried and got dressed, grabbed his Desert Eagle and slapped in a fresh clip. He grabbed the key to his new Yenko edition Camaro and ran out of the guest house, with murder on his mind.

***

Julie fell face forward, exhausted and out of breath after her second orgasm. She had gotten so hot and horny after the fiasco with the French guys that just miles away, she made Bucks pull over at a small grocery store, climbed over onto his lap with her skirt up, pantyhose ripped, thong to the side, and bounced on his dick reverse-cowgirl style, until she was feeling like she'd had enough.

Rock, used to his humans engaging in the loud and wild physical activity, laid on the GTO's back seat, not bothered at all.

Lil' Durk's "My Beyonce," featuring Dej Loaf, crooned through the speakers. Bucks wanted to stay like that. He loved how it felt to be inside her, especially while he sat behind the wheel of a pricey ol' school with over a million dollars' worth of cocaine in the trunk, and just under a million in cash.

"Baby, I fucking love you so much!" Julie said, getting emotional.

"I can't even believe we're gonna have a baby together, and we're engaged!"

"It's hittin' you, huh? It just got real?" Bucks asked, remembering when it all hit him.

"Yes! It's like, I'm seeing—"

Rock suddenly hopped up and started barking. He was looking out of the driver's side. Julie and Bucks turned and saw an SUV parked a few feet away from them, facing the GTO. Its bright headlights suddenly turned on, then the sound of the engine revving came.

"Shit! Hop off, bae!" Bucks urged Julie, as the vehicle shot forward, racing right at them.

Julie jumped off of him, scrambling to get back in her seat. Rock's bark turned demonic, seeing the vehicle speeding towards them. Julie grabbed her Night Hawk Custom 1911 .45 out of her handbag and put down her window. Bucks flew out of the parking lot, hopping onto the main road, and flooring it.

BOC! BOC! BOC! BOC! BOC! BOC!

Julie fired at the grille in attempts to take the radiator out, but saw her bullets pinged off of it. She realized it was bulletproof.

Bucks reached over and pulled her back inside right before he made a hard right turn. The SUV stayed on their bumper. Julie cursed as it sped up. Bucks swerved out of the way as it tried to ram them. The driver faked it and stayed in the lane it was in, then got alongside the GTO's passenger side.

Julie pointed her gun at the masked man behind the wheel. The driver stuck up the middle finger at her.

BOC! BOC! BOC!

Bulletproof windows as well. Julie wanted to unload the last of the clip, but knew it was pointless.

Bucks hit the brake pedal hard. The GTO skidded to a hard stop. The SUV kept going on, bending the corner at the next turn, and disappearing.

"What the hell was that?" Bucks asked, still sitting stopped in the middle of the street.

Julie gripped her .45 tightly in her hands, itching to tell him to go catch the son of a bitch. Rock's nose nudged her arm. He whimpered, feeling her anger.

"That was someone thinkin' we scare easily," she said back to him.

Bucks shook his head. "They gon' have to try harder than that," he said, though he most definitely was terrified, not for his sake, but because of the precious cargo he had in the seat next to him, who also was carrying precious cargo in her belly.

Chapter 16

Yvette smiled as she walked next to Alfonzo. He had taken her hand, after what seemed to her that he had been dying to take their dinner date a little further. She was glad to see that he was getting more comfortable with her, especially after she turned her phone off to stop T.G. from blowing her line up. She needed space, and if he wasn't going to take the hint, then she would force him to sit on a bag full of ice to keep a cool ass.

"Did you enjoy your dinner?" Alfonzo asked, as they walked to where a little gazebo sat, out in a quiet section of the property, by a pond.

"I did. I'm glad we came, 'Fonz," she told him, generally feeling peacefully happy.

They took seats on the bench inside. The sound of traffic from nearby Milwaukee Avenue, mixed with the bright lighting, and the coolness of the change in seasons put Yvette at ease, despite that little devil on her shoulder, telling her to go find T.G. and pistol whip him, then go find the sluts that touched what was hers, and give Sir some booty-meat treats.

"Can I be for real with you right now, Yvette?" Alfonzo asked, sitting so close to her that she could feel his body heat.

She looked directly into his eyes. "Yes."

"I been feelin' you since I first met you. I don't think that I have gone a single night without thinking about you since then. You're like, the epitome of a strong Black woman."

Yvette almost swooned over him. The look in his eyes had her feeling like she was in a spaceship, travelling through the galaxies, seeing all types of shit with bright colorful lights. The light in his eyes gave her an orgasmic feeling.

"You're sweet," she told him, feeling shy all of a sudden. "Why is you tryna' butter me up, 'Fonz? I'm your boss."

"The sexiest boss on the planet," he added, taking her hand and raising it to his lips, planting a soft kiss on it.

Yvette's nipples grew erect at how soft his lips felt. She so badly wanted to hike her skirt up, make him open her legs wide, rip a hole in her pantyhose, pull her thong off and suck her pussy with them shits.

"I have a man, 'Fonz," Yvette told him.

He smiled. "I know."

"So… you know I can't keep leadin' you on."

"You're not, I'm diggin' you and you're pissed at him, for whatever he did. You're seeking to alleviate some of the anger inside of you, so you agreed to come dine with me, maybe because you wanted to stay away from him, and enjoy a stress-free evening, with a handsome guy that has no ulterior motives."

Yvette was once again wowed by his words. He had just spoken her entire mind, and he did it, without breaking eye contact.

Before she even knew it, Yvette had leaned in and planted a kiss on his lips. It lasted for three seconds. She drew back, and they gazed into each other's eyes. Alfonzo licked his lips and smiled at her.

That was it. She grabbed his shirt, yanked him to her, and kissed him with an insatiable desire.

Yvette's temperature rose as they lip-boxed. With her eyes closed, she felt him, and his soul, kissing her back. Seconds later, she felt him parting her legs. His hand rested on her thigh, caressing it. Then it started moving up… further and further, until it was so close to her swollen center that if it got any closer, she was going to cum all over it.

"Can I have you, Yvette?" he asked, pulling back for a second, feeling how wet the crotch of her pantyhose was. "Just for tonight? And maybe the next morning?"

His low deep rasp had her so hot that she was clueless as to how she had not spontaneously combusted yet.

Alfonzo's hand found its way inside her stockings, and into her thong. The second she felt his fingers searching for her clitoris, Yvette lost all self-control.

"Yes! Shit, 'Fonz!" she moaned, feeling his fingers playing with it, stroking her clit like he'd already done it before. "I want you, too!"

"Tell me what you want, Yvette," he said, moving his lips to kiss on her neck, still playing with her pussy.

"I w-w-want you to f-f-fuuck me! Now!"

Alfonzo pulled his hand out of her tights. He put it to her lips and told her to taste herself. Yvette obeyed him. She took two fingers into her mouth, and sucked her honey from them

He took his fingers away, stood up, and undid his pants. Yvette's eyes went wide when she saw how hung he was. The bulge in his boxer briefs had her mouth watering. She grew even more aroused by how he was ready to get it on in a public setting. It told her that all he had on his mind was her, and she was loving it.

"Pull this dick out and put it in your mouth," Alfonzo told her, asserting his male dominance.

Yvette slid forward, putting herself right in front of him. She reached up and pulled his boxer briefs down. His hardness came right out like, *hello*!

Yvette wrapped her left hand around it and looked up into his eyes. She puckered her lips and moved in to plant a naughty kiss on the bulbous tip, when right at that moment…

CRACK!

Alfonzo went flying backwards, landing on his ass with his dick up in the air. Yvette screamed when she saw T.G. there, with a crazed look in his bloodshot eyes.

"Tre-Tremaine!" she gasped, trying to pull her skirt down.

"You dirty, nasty bitch!" T.G. grabbed her and snatched her up by the collar of her shirt. "You finna suck this bitch ass nigga's dick in public?"

"Tremaine! Let me go!" Yvette demanded, trying to pry his hands loose.

WHAM!

A thick tree branch smacked T.G. in the head. He yelped as pain exploded in his skull. His grip broke and he dropped Yvette.

Grabbing his head, he turned and saw the man his girl was about to top off, with the tree branch in his hands.

"Nigga, you are dead!" T.G. roared, then he rushed Alfonzo.

Alfonzo side-stepped the furious swings and swung the branch, hitting T.G. in his side hard. Yvette heard the loud crack. T.G. howled in pain when the tree branch broke a couple of his ribs. He fell to the ground, struggling to breathe. He looked up at the guy, then at Yvette, who had tears in her eyes.

"Come on, Yvette! We're leaving!" Alfonzo told her, grabbing her hand.

She looked down at T.G., the man she loved with all of her heart, on the ground, holding his side, fire in his eyes that had once been filled with love, for her. He grunted and groaned, in agonizing pain, but so angry at the same time.

"You just... gon' leave me, Y-Yvette?" he stammered.

"You left me the minute you put yo' dick in those hoes, in our guest house, Tremaine!" she wept.

"Come on, Yvette! Fuck him!" Alfonzo urged her.

"So that's i-it? You finna go suck that nigga's dick and give him my pussy?"

"I'm finna do what you did to me!" Yvette snapped.

Alfonzo pulled her away, ushering her towards her DBX.

"Yvette!"

She heard T.G. yelling for her.

"Yveette! I'm sorry, baby! Don't do this! Please, baby!"

Her tears started falling faster. He kept hollering for her, but Alfonzo refused to allow her to go back. She was suddenly filled with affliction. All of the good and bad times they had endured, together. All of the near-death experiences they had survived, together. The love they had made, the smiles they shared. Yvette was sobbing loudly by the time Alfonzo got her to her SUV. He got her keys and helped her up into the passenger's seat.

He hurried and jumped behind the wheel, fired up the engine, and dipped out of the parking lot, having absolutely no intention of letting her out of his sight, or not finishing, what she had started.

"It's gon' be okay, Yvette," Alfonzo told her, taking her hand into his. "I will not let that dickhead hurt you. I promise."

Yvette sighed and nodded her head. She pulled her hand from his and got her phone out of her bag to text the only person in the world that she knew would never betray her.

***

"Fuck!" T.G. winced in pain as he got up off the ground.

He watched his woman and her dinner-date, hop into the SUV he had dropped two hundred thousand on—so she could shit on all the other bitches that thought they were doing it—and peel off.

"I'ma kill that bitch ass nigga, then I'ma dog that dumb ungrateful hoe-bitch, Joe!" he said to himself.

"Get in line."

T.G. spun around with the quickness when he heard a woman's voice came from behind him. When he saw her, he almost went insane. But it wasn't her that had him seething.

"You!" he growled through clenched teeth, eyes locked onto the man like a Pit Bull being goaded by his owner.

"Yeah, yeah, it's me," the man said sarcastically. "Get over it. We're here for one reason, and one reason only, guy."

The woman spoke then. "We want your bitch, and her bitch, and their lieutenants… dead."

"Why in the hell would I help either one of y'all?" he asked.

"Other than the fact that you just caught the girl you love about to suck off a guy that works for her, at her and her lesbian lover's shelter?" he said, grinning evilly at T.G.

"Lesbian lover?" T.G. questioned in puzzlement.

"You didn't know your woman and her Chink friend bump cunts?" the woman asked him, with a smirk.

"N-no… but so what! Fuck, is y'all watchin' her that hard?"

"Yep," the guy said. "Hard enough to know that she was also sucking and fucking that Colombian drug lord, her and her lover."

Just to rub it in more, he pulled out his iPhone and showed T.G. flicks of Yvette and Julie, sucking and licking on Benicio's dick together, then letting him fuck them in every hole his dick could fit in, outside on an elevated stone deck of a huge mansion.

The pain and hurt that T.G. was feeling was nothing compared to the pain and hurt he was now dying to put onto Yvette and Julie, for kissing his bro's lips with her nasty mouth.

"Send me them flicks," T.G. demanded them.

"Sure. But first, you have to agree to help us out," the man said. "Do we have a deal?"

"And for the record, you can lie and say yes, then disappear if you want," the woman said, eyeing him, paying very close attention to his facial expression. She saw pure rage and despair. "We will find you, just like we keep doing."

"Only this time, we won't play with you anymore," the man said, concluding their double-teaming.

T.G. looked at them for a hard minute. Neither of them blinked an eye. If looks could kill, he'd be dead.

"Aight. Bet," T.G. said. "But before I kill that bitch, I get to beat her muhfuckin' face in."

"Uh… that would kill her… genius," the woman sassed.

"You can lay in on her a little, but the kill belongs to me," her husband said, no longer smirking, nor grinning.

T.G. nodded his head. "Okay. Uh… can y'all take me to the hospital?"

They both laughed at him.

"Sure," the man agreed. "Come on 'n follow us to the car, and we'll drop you at the ER. When they patch you up, you'll have a number to call. We better hear from you the moment you're discharged, or our agreement will be terminated."

"And so will you be," the woman added.

Bitch! Get off his dick! T.G. thought, holding his side tighter as he followed the two, looking at the lady's nice little ass in her sexy pants suit. *Come hop on mine, you know what they say, once yo' white ass goes black, everything else is whack!* he added to himself, making himself chuckle.

***

"Are you sure?" Julie asked, sitting up on the bed, ass naked and sweaty… again.

"Yeah," she heard Yvette say, through her broken-up voice. "I'll be okay."

"I can come to you, 'Vette. I can come right now, and you can come stay here with me and Bucks."

"No. I'm okay, JuJu. I was just lettin' you know what happened. You and Bucks enjoy your night, I'll see you tomorrow."

The call ended before Julie could even find out where Yvette was. Then she remembered their iPhones were linked by GPS.

"Everything aight with sis?" Bucks asked, laid out on the bed naked next to her.

Julie looked at him. She told him what Yvette told her. His eyes went wide in shock.

"Get the fuck outta here!"

"That's what she said, and my bitch ain't got no reason to get to cappin'."

Bucks jumped up and grabbed his phone. He called T.G. but got no answer. He called twice more, still no answer. He sent an urgent text, and even an email, demanding T.G. to hit his line ASAP.

"Bae, when I see yo' guy, I'ma hurt him for puttin' hands on her, Joe! On 'erythang I love!"

Bucks nodded. "Let's worry about that later, bae. Yvette's safe, and bro ain't dumb enough to keep on in the same night. We'll link up with her tomorrow, then I'ma holla at dog for that foul-ass shit. Bro know better than to lay hands on women that ain't targets."

"You better handle him then, Bernard, because if you don't, I will!" Julie declared, already visualizing herself putting one in T.G.'s head.

***

Yvette laid back and allowed him to open her legs wide. He planted soft kisses on her inner thighs, licking circles in spots close to her love box. He licked up her leaking juices, savoring her taste.

He had been waiting for this. Waiting for her, and she had no clue for how long. Alfonzo's lust for her was more than lust. It was need. He longed for her with the thirst of a man stuck in a desert dying for water. Her body was the cup, and her essence was the refreshing drink that he needed.

He slurped her juices up and started French kissing her swollen pussy lips. Yvette moaned, back arching, heart pounding in her chest. Alfonzo had her feeling so good at that moment. When she felt him parting her, right as he took her clit and put it in his mouth, Yvette almost went blind.

"Mmmmm, 'Fonzo! Shit! That feels so good!" she told him.

He moaned as he dined on her like she was a juicy steak, fresh off the grill. She leaked like a broken faucet, the harder he went. In a matter of minutes, Yvette reached her climax. She exploded, cumming all in his face, soaking it like her pussy was a Super Soaker water gun.

Alfonzo licked her clean, then stood, ready for her to please him. Yvette put him on his back, got on her knees, gripping his throbbing nine-inch cock, she hunched over him.

He watched her open her mouth and lower her head down. The blissful euphoric pleasure he felt the second his dick entered her mouth was enough to make his toes curl up so hard that they could all snap off.

Yvette took him all the way to the back of her throat with ease, going down to his balls. Alfonzo groaned as she sucked harder, as she made her way back up to the tip of his dick. She went back down, and at the base, started humming.

"Oohh, shit!" Alfonzo nearly jumped out of his skin when the vibration she created made his nuts tingle like bits of electricity was coursing through his sack.

Yvette giggled. She knew that would get him. She stopped humming and took his dick out of her mouth, jerking it with one hand while looking at him.

"You like this, handsome?" she asked, with her eyes fixed right onto his. "You like havin' a bad bitch like me, naked with heels on, sucking your dick?"

"Yeeesss! Now stop talking and put it back in your mouth!" he pleaded.

Yvette lowered back down and started deep-throating him again. Alfonzo groaned and cursed. She started going crazy, sucking, slurping his pre-cum, jerking him, licking his nuts. He sat up and palmed her ass as she made love to his dick with her mouth. He smacked on it, rubbed it, caressing her meaty cheeks. He put two fingers to her soaking wet pussy, got them wet, then went for it. He slipped his middle finger into her tight asshole and started finger-fucking it.

She went even harder then, turned on to no end by his finger inside her dookie-chute. She went nuts on him, up until she tasted more pre-cum. She could tell he was getting there, so she stopped, letting his dick go.

Repositioning herself, Yvette got on her back and opened her inner door for him, beckoning for him to enter. Alfonzo climbed on top and slid himself into her wetness.

Her warmth had his eyes roll to the back of his head. Her tight tunnel fit him like a glove. He was beyond glad that she didn't make him put a condom on. He wanted to feel the pussy. He heard how good it was and now, he was experiencing it firsthand.

Alfonzo pushed her legs out as wide as they could go and started jack-hammering the pussy. Yvette cried out at the top of her lungs as he filled her with mind-blowing bliss.

She exploded minutes later, cumming all over his dick.

He dropped to his side, pulled her to him, and lifted her right leg up. He went back inside and fucked her while she buried her face in his strong chest. He went deep, long stroking the pussy. Yvette couldn't help it. She bit his pectoral muscle hard. Alfonzo roared from the pain, but he didn't stop hitting it. He hit it harder as her teeth made marks in his flesh.

"Fuck!" he cursed, loving it.

Yvette let him go, then she took over. She pushed him onto his back, climbed aboard and mounted him. Holding his dick, she slid down on his pole, impaling herself.

Fuck going slow. She went ham on him right away. She bounced up and down on him, titties jumping, biting her bottom lip as she gripped his chest. Alfonzo sat up and buried his face in her chest, motorboating her breasts. She started laughing from the sensational tickle that pulsated in her melons, making her nipples tingle.

Yvette gave him her best. She cut loose. Her anger and resentment towards T.G., and her strong attraction to Alfonzo fueled her to focus on the man that was under her, and nobody else. He had all of her attention, and all of her mind, body, and soul.

She came all over him minutes later. Alfonzo took back over, got her in the doggy-style position and hit it from the back, while smacking on her ass, pulling her hair, talking hot and dirty shit to her.

Yvette buried her face in the bed and screamed as she erupted again. Alfonzo pulled his wet dick out of her pussy, gripped her sweaty booty cheeks, and spread them open. His dick swelled up when he feasted his eyes on her puckered asshole. It unpuckered a little as she looked back at him, with the sexiest fuck-face he had ever seen.

Alfonzo spit a wad of saliva onto her butthole and put the tip of his dick to it. He looked at her, while easing inside. He saw her eyes roll, lips curled up, hands clenching the bedsheet.

"You okay?" he asked, pausing for a second before going any further.

"Y-yeesss! Put it in, 'Fonz!"

He eased it in some more, then slow-stroked her ass. It took less than a minute for him to feel her unclench. She started throwing it back at him, while she looked back, locking eyes with him. He gritted his teeth, held onto her hips, and made her cum again in five minutes.

Yvette could feel his dick spasming inside her asshole. He was ready to bust a nut, and she wanted it to be the most memorable nut he ever had.

She reached back, grabbed it and pulled his dick out of her ass, then she got off the bed, dropping to her knees on the floor. Alfonzo followed, seeing what she wanted when she opened her mouth.

He put his dick in her mouth, loving how she wasn't bothered or grossed out by sucking his cock, right after it had been in her asshole.

This is a freak forreal! They were right! I'm cuffin' this hoe-bitch! And she got money, too! Alfonzo thought as Yvette allowed him to face-fuck her.

His balls slapped her chin. His dick went down her throat. He held her head in place, threw his head back, feeling his nut coming. As it rose, Alfonzo pulled his dick out of her mouth and started jerking it, inches away from her face. Seconds later, as Yvette stuck her tongue out, he exploded.

"F-fuuuuuuuck!" he roared, shooting hot globs of semen all over her face.

Yvette felt the splatters dripping down her face. She caught what she could on her tongue and swallowed his jizz, moaning as the taste of him made her want to go at him again.

"Holy shit!" Alfonzo exclaimed, amazed by how she didn't hold back a bit on their very first time.

She giggled, still on her knees before him. "I take it that you liked it, huh?"

"Maaaaan, I have never had a woman open up on me like that before in my life."

"Well, play your cards right, 'Fonz, and there will be plenty more times like that to follow," she told him. "Even out under a pavilion, or in a park, or in a movie theatre, filled with people."

His eyes went wide. "You would fuck in public like that?"

"Alfonzo, for the right man, I would give him the pussy in the middle of a traffic jam, because with the right one, I'll see nobody but him, and only him."

Alfonzo smiled down at her. "Then I am going to have to work hard to show you that I am that him that you should see and not that bastard who obviously had no clue what he just lost." He pulled her up from the floor, and ignoring all the cum on her face he kissed her, long and deep, making her hot all over again. A second later, he pulled back. He looked in her eyes then. "You are mine now, Yvette. Forget about that other guy."

She looked back into his eyes. She nodded her head, stuck in a daze by how powerful he seemed to her in that moment.

"Okay, baby. I'm yours, and you are mines," Yvette said. She grabbed his dick and squeezed it. "But right now, I'm your bitch, so treat me like it," she told him, then she sank back down to her knees, ready to go again, and maybe again after that.

Chapter 17

One Week Later…

Julie finished flat ironing her hair, then gave herself a onceover in her mirror. The dark, light, and bright blue DKNY long-sleeved wrap dress fit her body so perfectly. She wore nude pantyhose, and white DKNY stiletto pumps. Her glossy blue lips and her eyelids matched, along with the white-gold Tiffany & Co jewelry she had on, the custom Hublot on her wrist flicked with blue sapphires surrounding the blue dial.

She grabbed her iPhone and the keys to the 2021 Rolls-Royce Dawn that her fiancé bought for her a few days ago, and had it filled with red roses, and custom designed diamond jewelry.

Rock awaited her down in the massive foyer of her and Bucks's mansion. Excitedly, he ran to her as she came down the stairs, stepping onto glossy white Italian marble flooring.

"Ready to go, boy? Huh? You ready to go?" she asked, patting his head.

Rock sat and barked three times, tail wagging on the floor.

Julie went to grab her blue diamond-stitched DKNY handbag from the table centered under the big gold chandelier, when her phone rang in her hand.

"Sergeant Tran," she answered, grabbing her bag and heading to the front door.

"Hi, Sergeant Tran. How are you this morning, ma'am?" a male asked.

Julie opened the door and was hit with the cool brisk breeze. Rock trotted out before her but stayed close.

"I'm fine. Who is this?" Julie asked, closing the door behind her and heading towards the double-decker seven-car garage, sitting alongside their mansion.

"Oh me? I'm just a messenger, ma'am," he chuckled.

Julie stopped walking. "A messenger? Okay. Care to quit playin' games before I track you down and lock your ass up?"

He laughed again. "Believe me, Tran. This is not a game, you chink bitch. What it is, though, is your last day on earth. Do your best to enjoy it while you can. Buh-bye now."

The call ended, without a word more.

Rock trotted back up to Julie, sensing her change in moods. He barked at her, bringing her out of her stuck state. Immediately, she sent a text to Bucks, and one to Yvette about it. She didn't recognize the voice, but she was certain that had to be Webster that had just orchestrated the death threat.

She went into her bag and pulled out her new Night Hawk custom Korth NXR .44 Magnum, with a six-inch ventilated barrel.

"Keep those eyes open, Rock," Julie told her German killer, her own eyes shifting around her and Bucks's vast property, half expecting a pop up. "Muhfuckas steady thinkin' shits sweet, so we gon' have to show 'em... again."

The garage port door opened up when she hit the button. Sitting parked under an all-black Aston Martin DB11 Volante drop-top, was her two-door Rolls-Royce Dawn, its deep-sea blue pearl exterior gleaming hard, shining as if it had never seen a speck of dust.

Julie and Rock went and hopped into the white and wood-grain interior. The V12 engine purred when Julie push-started it. She backed out, about-faced, and turning on the music, bumping Doja Cat's "Can't Wait." She headed off to get on her way to get Yvette, with her revolver on her lap, and her back-up under her seat.

***

Yvette squealed in delight, raised up on the pointed toes of her red suede, knee-high Gucci stiletto boots. Leaned over the vanity sink in Alfonzo's bathroom, she had just finished putting on her glossy fire-engine red lipstick that went with her outfit, a black, long-sleeved Gucci sweater top, with red roses embroidered all over it, a black pleated leather Gucci skirt, and black pantyhose, with Gucci signs monogrammed into them. Alfonzo dressed in his normal casual attire, couldn't resist her when he walked in. The shape of her ass pulled him in like it had the strongest gravitational pull. Less than a minute after he had come in, he was on his knees behind her, with her skirt up, her pantyhose down, her thong to the side, and his face in her ass crack.

Yvette bit her bottom lip, moaning in bliss. The feeling of his tongue twirling around her asshole had her head spinning around and around, He ate her ass like it was the tastiest treat on earth. He stuck his tongue inside of it, making her toes curl up. She came out of her ass a minute later.

Alfonzo raised up then, dropped his jeans and slid his dick into her asshole. He gripped her wide hips, cursing and groaning, until he felt his balls tingling from his nut beginning to rise.

When he pulled his dick out, Yvette spun, dropped down, and opened her mouth wide, sticking her tongue out.

Alfonzo jerked his cock until he busted his nut. Hot globs shot out. Yvette caught his jizz in her mouth and swallowed it, licking her sexy red lips when he was done.

"Fuck! Goddamn, Yvette! Why can't I ever resist you?" he asked, pulling his boxer briefs and pants up, while she rose up and fixed her own clothes.

"Hmmm. Maybe because I'm beautiful, thick, a freak, and a Black queen, all rolled into one badass bitch?"

"Yeah. I think that about says it. I think I'ma have to wife you, baby."

Yvette laughed as she grabbed her black Gucci tote bag and iPhone. "Yo' ass need to learn how to cook first, them eggs you made got my stomach all the way fucked up."

She pulled him down to her and kissed him deeply, then turned on her heels to head out. Alfonzo gave her ass a smack, following behind her to the living room, where Sir was in his harness, ready to go.

"See you tonight, tiger," Yvette purred to him, then left out with her dog.

***

Outside, Yvette and Sir stood in the pick-up/drop-off section, waiting for Julie. Her stomach started bubbling. She groaned and farted. Sir looked at her and barked.

"Shut up, Sir! Blame the gas on 'Fonz eggs!" Yvette shot back, placing a hand on her gut as it continued bubbling.

Yvette saw the sleek blue drop-top turn into the half-rounded pick-up/drop-off section of the building. Rock stood up with his front paws on the side, barking and wagging his tail when he saw Sir.

Sir reciprocated the excitement of seeing his homie.

The suicide-style door opened when Julie hit the button. Sir climbed in and joined Rock in the rear. Yvette sat in the passenger's seat. The door closed automatically.

"No more threatenin' calls or texts?" Yvette asked her, still feeling her gut bubbling up.

"No.," Julie noticed how uncomfortable Yvette looked. "What's wrong?"

"I don't know. My stomach hurts, his ass made eggs, and I think they fuckin' with me."

A silent one slipped out. Yvette's eyes went wide, hoping Julie didn't smell it.

"Um… okay," Julie said, with puzzled brow. "Yo' ass better not get to pootin' in my car, or yo' ass finna walk."

***

They made a stop at the shelter to check on all the ladies and young girls. Yonnie lit up with glee when Yvette walked into her bedroom. Yvette hugged her with a warm motherly embrace, so very happy to see the young one. Sir was overjoyed to see Yonnie and Rock as well. Julie gushed over Yonnie. She found the little girl to be the most adorable little thing ever.

The chefs there made lunch for everyone. Roasted lamb chops, smothered in honey-barbecue sauce, cheese macaroni, sweet baked beans, and cornbread had everyone so full that nobody could move for at least an hour.

Yvette and Julie let their dogs use the bathroom out back, then hopping back into the Dawn, Julie headed off, driving them out to the station to catch up on boring paperwork.

***

"Heeeeey, look who's back!" Yvette shouted when she saw Lieutenant Michaels, sitting in his office.

"Boss man!" Julie screamed excitedly, running in to hug him, with Rock right behind her. She threw her arms around him and hugged him like a daughter that was anxiously waiting to pick her dad up from doing a lengthy prison bid. "I'm so glad you're back!"

Michaels smiled, chuckling deeply. He was definitely appreciative of the emphatic love.

"Nice to see you, too, Sergeant. Been hearing great things," he told her, as she let him go.

Yvette entered but stepped back out when she felt gas coming.

"So, how do you like light-duty, Miss Future Mother?" Michaels asked Julie.

"It sucks. I like beating people up," she replied.

Michaels busted out laughing. "You'll be able to do that again when you have the baby and get back into shape."

Yvette gasped. "Oooooo! Lieutenant! You don't supposed to tell a woman anything about gettin' in shape! Shame on you!"

Julie laughed.

"Hmm. Maybe that's why my niece got mad at me after she had her baby," Michaels said, remembering the day.

The ladies busted out laughing.

An urgent call came through Michaels's radio, requesting back up to assist in a high-speed chase on I-94, in the Gurnee area, very close to where they were.

"Gotta go, ladies!" Michaels hopped up, got his radio, firearm, and ran out, joining the other troopers, rushing out to get to the party.

Julie groaned, pissed that her light-duty status only allowed her to do office work, and check up on open cases.

"Don't worry, baby." Yvette kissed Julie's lips in secret, now that nobody was around. "I'll be with you on and off duty. Just make sure Bucks don't get all the goodie-good to himself," she said, giving Julie's perky ass a smack.

"You know I'll always get wet for you. Yvette," Julie replied. "But yo' ass better not give all the pussy to Mr. 'Fonzo's proper ass."

"Mmm-mm. See, he know how to lick it and stick it real good, but he's no JuJu Tran. Now, let's make moves. We gotta go pick that stuff up for ol' boy."

***

They shot down to Chicago's Humbolt Park neighborhood and picked up a duffel bag full of dirty guns, and a bag full of cash that was payment for the method Yvette and Julie used to get rid of dirties.

They took them out to a small storage space in Waukegan and melted the guns down to puddles. Afterwards, they went and collected cash that Bucks needed scooped from the list of clients he had. They brought him nearly ten million. Julie got a quickie in, then they got back to work, heading to follow up on a wreck that had claimed the life of a young college student en route to class, down by O'Hare Airport.

***

"I should've put a siren and strobe light on this fucking car, man," Julie said, frustrated to be stuck in grid-locked traffic on I-94, just past Lake Cook Road, south bound.

Yvette laughed. "A four hundred seventy-thousand-dollar convertible Rolls-Royce with a police siren and strobe lights? Now that would fuck all these niggas up, Joe."

They laughed as Post Malone and 21 Savage humped through the audio system, rapping about being rockstars.

Ten minutes later, traffic had barely moved. Julie logged into her police account and saw reports of an over-turned school bus, three miles up.

"That's a damn shame. Why is there so many accidents involving school buses these days, man? I'm so tired of hearin' little kids gettin' hurt and killed in senseless crashes."

"Me, too." Julie shook her head and sighed to herself.

***

Another ten minutes passed. Yvette's stomach started going crazy again, percolating, like a beaker with crack cooking up inside of it. She groaned as she felt her guts rolling.

"Oh, shit! JuJu! I need a bathroom! Like now!" she said urgently, feeling her bowels trying to release.

"How the hell do you expect me to do that, Yvette?" Julie asked, panicking her damn self, not wanting her exclusive white leather seats ruined.

"Beep the horn! Make this bitch next to us move! Get to the shoulder and goooo!" Yvette said through clenched teeth as she squeezed her legs closed and dug her heels into the floor.

Julie started hitting the horn, yelling for the lady in the Nissan on her right. She turned her head and saw Yvette hopping around in her seat, two dogs in the back, looking restless, and the Asian chick behind the wheel of the expensive automobile trying to get her attention.

The woman rolled her window down.

"Ma'am! We need to cut past you!" Julie yelled as Yvette started crying from the painful pressure building in her gut. "We have an emergency!"

"Sorry! Can't help you! I got an emergency too, honey!" the lady replied, so sarcastically that it pissed Yvette all the way off.

She grabbed her badge and her gun out of her handbag. She held her badge up and pointed her pistol at the woman.

"Bitch, get the fuck outta the way before I pop yo' ass!"

Fearing for her life, the woman slammed it into reverse and mashed the gas. She backed into an eighteen-wheeler behind her.

Julie hit the gas, swerving hard to the right. She shot over to the shoulder and made her Rolls-Royce ride like a Corvette, praying that nobody pulled out in front of her.

"Still think sirens and strobes would be dumb to have right now?" Julie yelled out as the wind blew over the windshield from her pushing past sixty miles an hour on the shoulder.

"JuJu! Shut the fuck up and... ssss... oooohhh... driiive!"

The exit ramp for Tahy Ave approached. Julie hurried off the highway, cut over the bridge where the bumper-to-bumper traffic was underneath, and swerved into a gas station on the corner. She slammed on the brakes when she got to the rear of the building where the bathroom was.

Yvette jumped out, leaving gas behind, running to the bathroom door cupping her ass, pleading that it was open.

"Fuuuck!" she screamed when she saw that it was locked.

A turd slipped out of her as she high tailed it to the store to get the key. She cringed, feeling the mush catch in her expensive tights.

"Bathroom! Key! Now!" Yvette pleaded to the clerk as another one started poking out.

The clerk tossed her the key. Yvette ran out of the store, but just as she stepped a foot outside…

BRRRRRRRR! BRRRRRRR!

BRRRRRRR! BRRRRRR!

She heard assault rifle gunfire, then she heard Julie screaming.

Her bowels exploded right then as she ran towards the back of the gas station. It spewed out of her like hot lava that refused to stay in the volcano any longer. She grimaced, disgusted by the mushiness under her. Waddling, groaning and cursing as so much of it flowed into her pantyhose, Yvette kept her feet moving. She bent the corner at the back of the building, and gasped when she saw Sir and Rock, laying in pools of blood, not moving. The Rolls-Royce's driver's door was open, but there was no Julie.

"Get the fuck off of meee!" Yvette heard Julie scream just then. She groaned as more flowed out of her. Doubling over in severe pain, Yvette looked further and saw Julie being dragged by two men, wearing black hooded sweat suits, with skull masks, and AK-47s strapped over their shoulders.

"Ju-JuJuuu!" Yvette screamed, as they threw her inside of an old black Chevy van.

Yvette forced herself to stand up and attempted to run.

WHAM!

"Aagghh!" she screamed, when something hard bashed her in the back of the head, opening up a gaping wound as she flew face forward to the ground.

Her head throbbed and felt like it was on fire. She heard the all-too-familiar sound of a shotgun being pumped.

"Hey. Excuse me, miss?"

Yvette's heart dropped when she heard his voice.

No... no... no... no... no... nooo... please! she thought.

She rolled over to her back and found herself looking up into Webster's demented eyes.

"Hi, Jones. Did you miss me?" he asked, holding the Mossberg in both of his hands, pointed at her face.

Yvette was speechless. She could barely see straight.

"Aww. You're bleeding. Here, lemme' get you some help," Webster said, then he whistled loudly.

Yvette heard a vehicle pull up and screech to a stop right by her head.

A pair of black Timberlands appeared by her face. She turned her head and looked up into T.G.'s eyes.

"Remember this guy?" she heard Webster ask. "Your ex-boyfriend, right, since you were about to swallow another man's cock in a public setting in front of him."

Yvette shitted herself even more.

"Put her in the van. People are looking," Webster told T.G., as he looked around, seeing crowds ducked behind cars, and running away.

T.G. snatched her up off the ground and went to toss her in the van. Yvette, filled with rage by T.G.'s tremendous betrayal, grabbed him and bit down on his right cheek as hard as she could.

He howled in pain as her teeth sank into his flesh. He tried to get her off. Yvette yanked her head hard, and ripped the skin off, exposing his teeth.

Blood spurted from the big hole. T.G. buckled to his knees, crying in agony, trying to hold his face.

She tried to run. Webster grabbed her by her hair and yanked her back to him.

"Get her in the damn van, Dale!" Yvette heard a woman yell.

Webster muscled her into the van and held her down while she tried so hard to get free. The next thing she knew, Yvette saw Samantha and Bernice, in the front seats of the van.

What the fuck? she thought, beyond bewildered that they were all at her and Julie.

T.G. staggered into the van, holding his bleeding face. He slammed the door shut as Samantha hit the gas and shot up out of the gas station.

"Whew! Holy shit! She reeks!" Samatha said, rolling her window down. "Your man went a little too far with that bubble-gut powder, Dale."

Yvette, still trying to fight, heard what the woman said. Her eyebrows furrowed, puzzled by the comment.

"Did the trick, though, babe," Yvette heard Webster say.

Yvette looked over at T.G., sitting in the corner, holding a towel to his face. Her eyes filled with tears. Realization of the man she had loved with every ounce of her, had just played a role in putting her in the hands of her enemy.

"How could you?" she wept to him.

"Quite easily," Webster said.

She looked back up at him, right as he brought a rag drenched in chloroform down over her nose. "It'll all be over soon, Jones. You and Tran will be reunited soon, down in the fiery underworld... forever."

Yvette's vision blurred as the strong chloroform disoriented her, then seconds later, everything went dark... then black...

To Be Continued

194

Lock Down Publications and Ca$h Presents
Assisted Publishing Packages

Due to an increase in the price of services we have increased our prices. The prices below reflect the price increase as of 11/1/24.

BASIC PACKAGE **$699** Editing Cover Design Formatting	**UPGRADED PACKAGE** **$1000** Typing Editing Cover Design Formatting Upload eBooks to Amazon Upload Paperback to Amazon
ADVANCE PACKAGE **$1,400** Typing Editing (line editing/content) Cover Design Formatting Copyright Registration Proofreading Upload eBooks to Amazon Upload Paperback to Amazon	**LDP SUPREME PACKAGE** **$1,700** Typing Editing (line editing/content) Cover Design Formatting Copyright Registration Proofreading Set up Amazon Account Upload eBooks to Amazon Upload Paperback to Amazon Advertise on LDP's Amazon and Facebook Page

***Other services available upon request.
Additional charges may apply

Lock Down Publications
P.O. Box 944
Stockbridge, GA 30281-9998
Phone: 470 303-9761
Email: lockdownpublications@gmail.com

Submission Guideline

Submit the first three chapters of your completed manuscript to ldpsubmissions@gmail.com. In the subject line add **Your Book's Title**. The manuscript must be in a Word Doc file and sent as an attachment. Document should be in Times New Roman, double spaced, and in size 12 font. Also, provide your synopsis and full contact information. If sending multiple submissions, they must each be in a separate email.

Have a story but no way to send it electronically? You can still submit to LDP/Ca$h Presents. Send in the first three chapters, written or typed, of your completed manuscript to:

LDP: Submissions Dept
P.O. Box 944
Stockbridge, GA 30281-9998

DO NOT send original manuscript. Must be a duplicate.
Provide your synopsis and a cover letter containing your full contact information.

Thanks for considering LDP and Ca$h Presents.

NEW RELEASES

BLOODLINE OF A SAVAGE 1,2&3
THESE VICIOUS STREETS 1,2&3
RELENTLESS GOON
RELENTLESS GOON 2
BY PRINCE A. TAUHID

THE BUTTERFLY MAFIA 1-3
BY FUMIYA PAYNE

A THUG'S STREET PRINCESS 1,2&3
BY MEESHA

CITY OF SMOKE 1& 2
BY MOLOTTI

STEPPERS 1,2&3
THE REAL BADDIES OF CHI-RAQ
BY KING RIO

THE LANE 1&2
BY KEN-KEN SPENCE

THUG OF SPADES 1,2&3
LOVE IN THE TRENCHES 2
CORNER BOY CHRONICLES
BY COREY ROBINSON

TIL DEATH 3
BY ARYANNA

THE BIRTH OF A GANGSTER 4
BY DELMONT PLAYER

CHRISTOPHER "DIESEL" HORNEZES

PRODUCT OF THE STREETS 1&2
BY DEMOND "MONEY" ANDERSON

NO TIME FOR ERROR
BY KEESE

MONEY HUNGRY DEMONS 1,2&3
BY TRANAY ADAMS

HUNGRY FOR MONEY 1&2
BY SLIMBOS

A THUGGISH PASSION
KILLAZ ON STANDBY 1&2
LAND OF DA HOOLIGANZ 1,2&3
FRESH OFF DA PORCH
BY IRA B.

COUNTDOWN OF A KILLA 1&2
GUNS DOWN, BOTTOMS UP 1&2
SEX, MURDA AND GOD
BY LO-LIFE

THE LEVEL UP 1&2
BY LUXURY KING

FO'EVA ROLLIN' 1&2
BY ASSA RAYMOND BAKER

HUB CITY MENACE 1&2
BY J. WHITE

KILLA CREW
DYING FOR LIKES
BY ARYANNA

BAD B*TCHES WIT' GUNZ

IF YOU CROSS ME ONCE 6
ANGEL 5
By Anthony Fields

IMMA DIE BOUT MINE 5
By Aryanna

A THUGS STREET PRINCESS 3
EMBRACING THE LOVE OF A BOSS
By Meesha

PRODUCT OF THE STREETS 3
By Demond Money Anderson

STANDING ON HER BUSINESS
BY DG SANTANA

GET IT IN SLUGS 1&2
B. STALLS

CORNER BOYS 2
By Corey Robinson

THE MURDER QUEENS 6&7
By Michael Gallon

CITY OF SMOKE 3
By Molotti

CONFESSIONS OF A DOPEBOY
By Nicholas Lock

TENDER
BY KHUFU

CHRISTOPHER "DIESEL" HORNEZES

THA TAKEOVER
By Keith Chandler

BETRAYAL OF A G 2
By Ray Vinci

CRIME BOSS 4
By Playa Ray

Coming Soon from Lock Down Publications/Ca$h Presents

RAN OFF ON THE PLUG 2 by **PAPER BOI RARI**
STREET REDEMPTION by **TONY DANIELS**
SAVAGE FAMILY EMPIRE by **PRINCE TAUHID**
BAD BITCHES WIT' GUNZ by **DIESEL**
THE SINGLE LADIES by **DIESEL**
COKE BY THE TRUCKLOAD by **DIESEL**
PROBLEM SOLVED by **DIESEL**
TIPPIN' THE SCALES by **DIESEL**
OPPS CRY TOO by **SAYNOMORE**
A GANGSTA'S KARMA by **FLAME**

AVAILABLE NOW

RESTRAINING ORDER 1 & 2
By **CA$H & Coffee**

LOVE KNOWS NO BOUNDARIES 1-3
By **Coffee**

RAISED AS A GOON I, II, III & IV
BRED BY THE SLUMS I, II, III
BLAST FOR ME I & II
ROTTEN TO THE CORE I II III
A BRONX TALE I, II, III
DUFFLE BAG CARTEL I II III IV V VI
HEARTLESS GOON I II III IV V
A SAVAGE DOPEBOY I II
DRUG LORDS I II III
CUTTHROAT MAFIA I II
KING OF THE TRENCHES
By **Ghost**

LAY IT DOWN I & II
LAST OF A DYING BREED I II
BLOOD STAINS OF A SHOTTA I & II III
By **Jamaica**

LOYAL TO THE GAME I II III
LIFE OF SIN I, II III
By **TJ & Jelissa**

IF LOVING HIM IS WRONG…I & II
LOVE ME EVEN WHEN IT HURTS I II III
By **Jelissa**

BAD B*TCHES WIT' GUNZ

PUSH IT TO THE LIMIT
By **Bre' Hayes**

BLOODY COMMAS I & II
SKI MASK CARTEL I, II & III
KING OF NEW YORK I II, III IV V
RISE TO POWER I II III
COKE KINGS I II III IV V
BORN HEARTLESS I II III IV
KING OF THE TRAP I II
By **T.J. Edwards**

WHEN THE STREETS CLAP BACK I & II III
THE HEART OF A SAVAGE I II III IV
MONEY MAFIA I II
LOYAL TO THE SOIL I II III
By **Jibril Williams**

A DISTINGUISHED THUG STOLE MY HEART I - III
LOVE SHOULDN'T HURT I II III IV
RENEGADE BOYS 1-4
PAID IN KARMA 1-3
SAVAGE STORMS 1-3
AN UNFORESEEN LOVE 1-3
BABY, I'M WINTERTIME COLD 1-3
A THUG'S STREET PRINCESS 1&2
By **Meesha**

CUM FOR ME 1-8
An LDP Erotica Collaboration

BLOOD OF A BOSS 1-5
SHADOWS OF THE GAME
TRAP BASTARD
By **Askari**

CHRISTOPHER "DIESEL" HORNEZES

A GANGSTER'S CODE 1-3
A GANGSTER'S SYN 1-3
THE SAVAGE LIFE 1-3
CHAINED TO THE STREETS 1-3
BLOOD ON THE MONEY 1-3
A GANGSTA'S PAIN 1-3
BEAUTIFUL LIES AND UGLY TRUTHS
CHURCH IN THESE STREETS
By **J-Blunt**

THE STREETS BLEED MURDER 1-3
THE HEART OF A GANGSTA 1-3
By **Jerry Jackson**

WHEN A GOOD GIRL GOES BAD
By **Adrienne**

THE COST OF LOYALTY 1-3
By **Kweli**

BRIDE OF A HUSTLA 1-3
THE FETTI GIRLS 1-3
CORRUPTED BY A GANGSTA 1-4
BLINDED BY HIS LOVE
THE PRICE YOU PAY FOR LOVE 1-3
DOPE GIRL MAGIC 1-3
By **Destiny Skai**

A KINGPIN'S AMBITION
A KINGPIN'S AMBITION II
I MURDER FOR THE DOUGH
By **Ambitious**

A DOPEBOY'S PRAYER
By **Eddie "Wolf" Lee**

BAD B*TCHES WIT' GUNZ

TRUE SAVAGE 1-7
DOPE BOY MAGIC 1-3
MIDNIGHT CARTEL 1-3
CITY OF KINGZ 1&2
NIGHTMARE ON SILENT AVE
THE PLUG OF LIL MEXICO 1&2
CLASSIC CITY
By **Chris Green**

LOVE & CHASIN' PAPER
By **Qay Crockett**

THE KING CARTEL 1-3
By **Frank Gresham**

THESE NIGGAS AIN'T LOYAL 1-3
By **Nikki Tee**

GANGSTA SHYT 1-3
By **CATO**

THE ULTIMATE BETRAYAL
By **Phoenix**

BOSS'N UP 1-3
By **Royal Nicole**

I LOVE YOU TO DEATH
By **Destiny J**

BROOKLYN HUSTLAZ
By **Boogsy Morina**

GANGSTA CITY
By **Teddy Duke**

TO DIE IN VAIN
SINS OF A HUSTLA
By **ASAD**

I RIDE FOR MY HITTA
I STILL RIDE FOR MY HITTA
By **Misty Holt**

A GANGSTER'S REVENGE 1-4
THE BOSS MAN'S DAUGHTERS 1-5
A SAVAGE LOVE 1&2
BAE BELONGS TO ME 1&2
A HUSTLER'S DECEIT 1-3
WHAT BAD BITCHES DO 1-3
SOUL OF A MONSTER 1-3
KILL ZONE
A DOPE BOY'S QUEEN 1-3
TIL DEATH 1-3
IMMA DIE BOUT MINE 1-5
By **Aryanna**

BROOKLYN ON LOCK 1 & 2
By **Sonovia**

A DRUG KING AND HIS DIAMOND 1-3
A DOPEMAN'S RICHES
HER MAN, MINE'S TOO 1&2
CASH MONEY HO'S
THE WIFEY I USED TO BE 1&2
PRETTY GIRLS DO NASTY THINGS
By **Nicole Goosby**

THE STREETS ARE CALLING
By **Duquie Wilson**

BAD B*TCHES WIT' GUNZ

LIPSTICK KILLAH 1-3
CRIME OF PASSION 1-3
FRIEND OR FOE 1-3
By **Mimi**

TRAPHOUSE KING 1-3
KINGPIN KILLAZ 1-3
STREET KINGS 1&2
PAID IN BLOOD 1&2
CARTEL KILLAZ 1-3
DOPE GODS 1&2
By **Hood Rich**

STEADY MOBBN' 1-3
THE STREETS STAINED MY SOUL 1-3
By **Marcellus Allen**

WHO SHOT YA 1-3
SON OF A DOPE FIEND 1-4
HEAVEN GOT A GHETTO 1&2
SKI MASK MONEY 1&2
By **Renta**

GORILLAZ IN THE BAY 1-4
TEARS OF A GANGSTA 1/&2
3X KRAZY 1&2
STRAIGHT BEAST MODE 1&2
By **DE'KARI**

TRIGGADALE 1-3
MURDA WAS THE CASE 1-3
By **Elijah R. Freeman**

MARRIED TO A BOSS 1-3
By **Destiny Skai & Chris Green**

CHRISTOPHER "DIESEL" HORNEZES

SLAUGHTER GANG 1-3
RUTHLESS HEART 1-3
By **Willie Slaughter**

GOD BLESS THE TRAPPERS 1-3
THESE SCANDALOUS STREETS 1-3
FEAR MY GANGSTA 1-5
THESE STREETS DON'T LOVE NOBODY 1-2
BURY ME A G 1-5
A GANGSTA'S EMPIRE 1-4
THE DOPEMAN'S BODYGAURD 1&2
THE REALEST KILLAZ 1-3
THE LAST OF THE OGS 1-3
By **Tranay Adams**

KINGZ OF THE GAME 1-7
CRIME BOSS 1-4
By **Playa Ray**

FUK SHYT
By **Blakk Diamond**

DON'T F#CK WITH MY HEART 1&2
By **Linnea**

ADDICTED TO THE DRAMA 1-3
IN THE ARM OF HIS BOSS
By **Jamila**

LOYALTY AIN'T PROMISED 1&2
By **Keith Williams**

FOREVER GANGSTA 1&2
GLOCKS ON SATIN SHEETS 1&2
By **Adrian Dulan**

BAD B*TCHES WIT' GUNZ

YAYO 1-4
A SHOOTER'S AMBITION 1&2
BRED IN THE GAME
By **S. Allen**

TRAP GOD 1-3
RICH $AVAGE 1-3
MONEY IN THE GRAVE 1-3
CARTEL MONEY
By **Martell Troublesome Bolden**

TOE TAGZ 1-4
LEVELS TO THIS SHYT 1&2
IT'S JUST ME AND YOU
By **Ah'Million**

KINGPIN DREAMS 1-3
RAN OFF ON DA PLUG
By **Paper Boi Rari**

THE STREETS MADE ME 1-3
By **Larry D. Wright**

CONFESSIONS OF A GANGSTA 1-4
CONFESSIONS OF A JACKBOY 1-3
CONFESSIONS OF A HITMAN
By **Nicholas Lock**

I'M NOTHING WITHOUT HIS LOVE
SINS OF A THUG
TO THE THUG I LOVED BEFORE
A GANGSTA SAVED XMAS
IN A HUSTLER I TRUST
By **Monet Dragun**

CHRISTOPHER "DIESEL" HORNEZES

QUIET MONEY 1-3
THUG LIFE 1-3
EXTENDED CLIP 1&2
A GANGSTA'S PARADISE
By **Trai'Quan**

CAUGHT UP IN THE LIFE 1-3
THE STREETS NEVER LET GO 1-3
By **Robert Baptiste**

NEW TO THE GAME 1-3
MONEY, MURDER & MEMORIES 1-3
By **Malik D. Rice**

THE LIFE OF A HOOD STAR
By **Ca$h & Rashia Wilson**

THE STREETS WILL NEVER CLOSE 1-4
By **K'ajji**

LIFE OF A SAVAGE 1-4
A GANGSTA'S QUR'AN 1-4
MURDA SEASON 1-3
GANGLAND CARTEL 1-3
CHI'RAQ GANGSTAS 1-4
KILLERS ON ELM STREET 1-3
JACK BOYZ N DA BRONX 1-3
A DOPEBOY'S DREAM 1-3
JACK BOYS VS DOPE BOYS 1-3
COKE GIRLZ
COKE BOYS
SOSA GANG 1&2
BRONX SAVAGES
BODYMORE KINGPINS
BLOOD OF A GOON
By **Romell Tukes**

BAD B*TCHES WIT' GUNZ

CREAM 2-3
THE STREETS WILL TALK
By **Yolanda Moore**

CONCRETE KILLA 1-3
VICIOUS LOYALTY 1-3
By **Kingpen**

THE ULTIMATE SACRIFICE 1-6
KHADIFI
IF YOU CROSS ME ONCE 1-5
ANGEL 1-4
IN THE BLINK OF AN EYE
By **Anthony Fields**

NIGHTMARES OF A HUSTLA 1-3
BLOOD AND GAMES 1&2
By **King Dream**

HARD AND RUTHLESS 1&2
MOB TOWN 251
THE BILLIONAIRE BENTLEYS 1-3
REAL G'S MOVE IN SILENCE
By **Von Diesel**

MOB TIES 1-7
SOUL OF A HUSTLER, HEART OF A KILLER 1-3
GORILLAZ IN THE TRENCHES
By **SayNoMore**

BODYMORE MURDERLAND 1-3
THE BIRTH OF A GANGSTER 1-4
By **Delmont Player**

FOR THE LOVE OF A BOSS 1&2
By **C. D. Blue**

KILLA KOUNTY 1-5
By **Khufu**

MOBBED UP 1-4
THE BRICK MAN 1-5
THE COCAINE PRINCESS 1-10
STEPPERS 1-3
SUPER GREMLIN 1-4
By **King Rio**

MONEY GAME 1&2
By **Smoove Dolla**

A GANGSTA'S KARMA 1-4
By **FLAME**

KING OF THE TRENCHES 1-3
By **GHOST & TRANAY ADAMS**

QUEEN OF THE ZOO 1&2
By **Black Migo**

GRIMEY WAYS 1-3
BETRAYAL OF A G
By **Ray Vinci**

XMAS WITH AN ATL SHOOTER
By **Ca$h & Destiny Skai**

KING KILLA 1&2
By **Vincent "Vitto" Holloway**

BETRAYAL OF A THUG 1&2
By **Fre$h**

BAD B*TCHES WIT' GUNZ

THE MURDER QUEENS 1-6
By **Michael Gallon**

FOR THE LOVE OF BLOOD 1-4
By **Jamel Mitchell**

HOOD CONSIGLIERE 1&2
NO TIME FOR ERROR
By **Keese**

PROTÉGÉ OF A LEGEND 1&2
LOVE IN THE TRENCHES 1&2
By **Corey Robinson**

THE PLUG'S RUTHLESS DAUGHTER 1&2
By **Tony Daniels**

BORN IN THE GRAVE 1-3
CRIME PAYS 1&2
By **Self Made Tay**

MOAN IN MY MOUTH
By **XTASY**

TORN BETWEEN A GANGSTER AND A
GENTLEMAN
By **J-BLUNT & Miss Kim**

HERE TODAY GONE TOMORROW 1&2
By **Fly Rock**

PILLOW PRINCESS
By **S. Hawkins**

SANCTIFIED AND HORNY
by **XTASY**

213

WOMEN LIE MEN LIE 1-4
FIFTY SHADES OF SNOW 1-3
STACK BEFORE YOU SPLURGE
GIRLS FALL LIKE DOMINOES
NAÏVE TO THE STREETS
By **ROY MILLIGAN**

LOYALTY IS EVERYTHING 1-3
CITY OF SMOKE 1&2
By **Molotti**

THE BUTTERFLY MAFIA 1-4
SALUTE MY SAVAGERY 1&2
By **Fumiya Payne**

THE LANE 1&2
By **Ken-Ken Spence**

THE PUSSY TRAP 1-5
By **Nene Capri**

DIRTY DNA
By **Blaque**

BOOKS BY LDP'S CEO, CA$H

TRUST IN NO MAN
TRUST IN NO MAN 2
TRUST IN NO MAN 3
BONDED BY BLOOD
SHORTY GOT A THUG
THUGS CRY
THUGS CRY 2
THUGS CRY 3
TRUST NO BITCH
TRUST NO BITCH 2
TRUST NO BITCH 3
TIL MY CASKET DROPS
RESTRAINING ORDER
RESTRAINING ORDER 2
IN LOVE WITH A CONVICT
LIFE OF A HOOD STAR
XMAS WITH AN ATL SHOOTER